DRIFTER
PART THREE

D1293491

A SAM PRICHARD MYSTERY

DRIFTER

PART THREE

DAVID ARCHER

USA TODAY BESTSELLING AUTHOR

"...THE NEXT JACK REACHER!"

PROLOGUE

Harry came walking into the restaurant, and Sam waved to show him where they were sitting. He waved back and made his way through the tightly packed tables to get to theirs, and sat down. He looked at Sam's empty dishes and blinked.

"Tell me they have steaks here," he said, and Sam laughed.

"Get the fillet of beef, Harry. I had it last night and it's incredible."

Harry placed the order when the waiter appeared, and then Sam and Ken began filling him in on the plan to hit Chandler that afternoon. Harry asked a few questions, nodded at the right places, and finally said, "Sounds to me like the best way to go about it. When you call Natasha, tell her we need a third machine pistol, though."

Ken scowled. "Harry, I'm going in alone, I already

explained that to you."

Harry looked at him. "Did I say anything different? I simply want to be armed, in case the bastard gets past you and comes running my way. Do you blame me?"

They took Harry's bag up to their room when he'd finished eating, and he took the chance to lie down for a short nap on the couch. They were scheduled to meet with Natasha there at the room at two, so Sam and Ken went and shared the bed for a couple of hours themselves. When they rose at one thirty, they found Harry up and using a laptop computer to study the area around the restaurant.

"I've got it all figured out," he said. "I see how you want to handle this, Ken, and I think it could work, but look at this: here, right to the north of the restaurant, there's this little narrow alley. It's just about wide enough for us to hide in single file, and it's invisible from the street. I'm thinking that if Sam and I were in there, then when you go in from the south end, we could strike from the opposite side. They wouldn't know for at least a few seconds what hit them, so we'd have a good chance of making the hit and coming out of it with all of us alive."

Ken stared at him. "You're not gonna let me do this my way, are you, you old bastard?"

Harry grinned at him. "I've been in this business a lot longer than you, son, remember that? Besides, there are times when you just have to do something, and I'm having one of those times. I need to be in on this, Ken.

Just deal with an old man's stubbornness, okay?"

Sam laughed. "You can't beat him, Ken, you might as well just face it. We're all going to be in on this, and it's gonna be better that way."

The three of them talked over the plan until they were all sure of what was expected of each of them, and by the time Natasha showed up, they were ready to get rolling. She gave Harry a hug, and kissed his cheek, then handed him the machine pistol he'd demanded.

They piled into her car, and she drove them to the restaurant so that they could all get into position. They knew that it would be a long wait, but they felt better about being there early, and each of them had spent long hours waiting before. It wasn't anything new to them, and they were all able to find a way to get comfortable.

Ken sat on a rock behind a bush that was about twenty yards from the place, while Harry and Sam had to sit down on the ground. Each of them had an earpiece in that Natasha had provided, so that when the surveillance team saw Chandler coming their way, they would be notified a few minutes early. That way, they could all get to their feet and be ready to move once their prey was all inside.

That call came at four forty, and the three of them readied themselves. One of the watchers confirmed that Chandler was in the car when it pulled up in front of the restaurant, and that he did get out and enter the place. Harry held up a hand to keep Sam from moving too quickly, and then he motioned for them to go.

They came around the north side of the entrance just as Ken came around from the south, and all three of them saw the group of men that was sitting at the table in the back. Chandler looked up at them, and his face registered shock at the site of Ken and Sam, and then Sam raised his gun and began firing. Chandler and his own men began shooting back, and Sam saw Chandler drop to the floor, and then Harry came around him, and everything was happening fast.

There were several other people in the restaurant, and they all began screaming and trying to run, and Sam was shoved aside by a man who was holding a child. He caught his balance, and leveled his gun once more, but then another man ran into him and he fell to one side. He hit a table, and slid off of it to the floor, and for a split second he was looking Chandler in the eye, but before he could even react, there was a foot coming down on his face. He pushed it off, and a man fell beside him, but Sam was fighting his way back to his feet. He tried to move forward, to get to Chandler, but a burst of gunfire came at him out of nowhere, and he ducked instinctively.

Something hit him again, and he fell onto another table, but by the time he could get up and see what was going on, the place where Chandler had been was empty. Four of his men were down, including David Glenn, but Chandler was gone. Sam spun around, looking for Ken, and saw him on the floor, his shirt covered in blood. He started toward him, but stepped on something, and when he looked down, he saw that he was stepping on Harry.

There was a bloody spot on Harry's face, and as Sam looked at him, he saw that blood was oozing out of it. Harry's mouth was working, but there was an odd look in his eyes, and Sam suddenly forgot about Chandler, forgot about Ken. He dropped to his knees and pulled the old man up to himself, and listened to see what Harry was saying, but it was too faint.

He looked down at the old man, and as he did, a blankness came over his eyes, and Sam stared at him.

He looked up and saw Ken, who was trying to get to a sitting position, and then he heard the sirens. He looked back down at Harry's lifeless face, and suddenly wondered if maybe Chandler really was the Beast.

And then he began to cry.

1

The sirens seemed to be everywhere, as more and more of the Israeli police began to swarm the little restaurant. It seemed like half of them didn't know how to shut their sirens off, but merely left the cars sitting there with the sirens screaming. Sam had been helped on to his feet, while paramedics loaded Harry onto a stretcher and rushed him out of the building. Another couple of paramedics had Ken sitting in a chair while they went over him, but he was trying to brush them off.

"Just who are you, Mr. Davis?" Sam looked up at the man who had asked the question.

"I already told you," Sam said. "I'm Jim Davis, an American tourist. My friends and I stopped in here for a bite to eat, and apparently we walked into a gunfight."

The man who was questioning him looked around at the carnage in the little restaurant, then looked back at

Sam. "My name is Boaz Ben Yazdi," he sa
Inspector with Israeli Police. I have spoken
tourists, from many countries including th.
States. Only very seldom do I find tourists
automatic pistols like these that I find all arou.
Can you explain to me where they came from?"

"Inspector," Sam said, "like I told you, we walked
into some sort of a gun battle. There were several men
on each side who were shooting, and then, just as
suddenly as it began, some of them ran out and got into
cars and raced away. That's all I know."

Ken caught his eye and gave an almost
imperceptible nod. This was the story they had practiced
and agreed on, just in case things went bad. From Sam's
point of view, things had just gone far worse than they
ever could have expected.

Ben Yazdi smiled at him. "Of course, that's what you
told me. But, you know, that leaves me wondering —
here we have four men dead, and all of them are holding
firearms of one sort or another, but for the other side,
you're telling me they all ran out unharmed. Is that
correct?"

Sam grinned. "Actually, now that you mention it, I
remember that they picked up one man who had fallen
and wasn't moving, and one of them was helping another
man who looked like he might've been shot in the leg."

Ben Yazdi nodded at this, and his smile grew even
wider. "Ah, yes, now it makes more sense. The attackers

...eir wounded and dead with them. Is that right?"

"Well, I guess that's how it looked."

"Mr. Davis," Ben Yazdi said, "even before we began to speak, I knew that you were not who you claim to be. Too many of the patrons here saw you with a machine pistol in your hand, so it is rather apparent to me that you are one of the combatants in this altercation. When I add to this information the fact that there is a record of your arrival on a diplomatic flight from the United States, even though neither you nor your friends are listed on any diplomatic roster, it becomes rather clear to me that I'm dealing with what must be special agents of an American task force. The only question that remains unanswered to me, then, is why such agents are here. Now, you can tell me, or I can simply detain you until I get the answers I seek. And incidentally, since you are not on any diplomatic roster, if it turns out that I'm correct in my assumptions then it is highly likely that you will be spending a great deal of time here in Israel. I can't say that you'll get to enjoy much in the way of tourism, and the accommodations might not be as luxurious as they are in the King David Hotel, but at least you'll get three meals each day. Well, most days."

There was a slight commotion near the entrance of the restaurant, and Ben Yazdi turned to see what was causing it. A blonde woman could be seen arguing with one of the constables who was standing outside, holding what appeared to be an ID case up in front of his face and pointing to it. The inspector gave a sigh of resignation. "Well, Mr. Davis," he said, without looking back at Sam. "It appears that your cavalry has arrived. If you had told me I would be dealing with Natasha Minsky today, I might very well have simply let you go. Since you didn't see fit to warn me, however, I might now consider it an insult that requires retribution." He glanced at Sam, and then put on smile as Natasha approached them.

"Inspector," Natasha said, "it seems that some of my new aides blundered into some sort of trouble, here. That's unfortunate, since I was just in the process of adding them to my unit roster."

Ben Yazdi took her hand, bent low over it and kissed it gently. When he stood, there was a twinkle in her eye, but the smile on his face remained as cold as ever. "Natasha," he said. "As always, it is a pleasure to see you again. I'm assuming that you're going to give me some reasonable explanation for all of this?"

Natasha laughed delightedly. "Oh, good heavens, no," she said. "How could I possibly have an explanation? The only reason I even know that something happened is because I was scheduled to join them here for dinner. You can imagine my surprise when I got a call from our embassy saying they had overheard your dispatchers saying that there had been a gun battle here. Well, I just had to come and see for myself what was going on."

"In that case, I'm going to hazard a guess that these

new aides of yours would be Mr. Davis, Mr. Clark and the unfortunate Mr. Milner, who just left in the ambulance. Would I be right?"

"Indeed, you would. They just arrived yesterday, and I was getting all the paperwork done today. I don't know why they were so lucky as to walk into this situation — I'm too busy being thankful that I was running late. Why, it might've been me who was taken away in the ambulance."

"Yes. So," Ben Yazdi said, "what you're telling me, then, is that all three of the men are part of your diplomatic mission, and therefore possess diplomatic immunity. Is that correct?"

"Why, yes, I suppose that is how it turns out. I do hope this won't cause any hard feelings between us."

"Oh, Natasha, we both know that it will. Why pretend otherwise? On the other hand, you're saving me from a great deal of paperwork, for all I need do now is report that the three individuals the witnesses all have stated were involved in the attack on these people could not possibly have been involved, since they are all low-level aides to an American diplomatic mission that deals with tourists who run into financial problems. That solves so many problems for me. How can I thank you?"

Natasha smiled and patted him on the cheek. "We can talk about that the next time you have an evening free, Boaz," she said. "How long has it actually been since you took me to dinner? I think it's a couple of months now, isn't it?"

Ben Yazdi nodded, his smile still as cold as it had been. "At least that long," he said. "Perhaps this Friday night?"

"Why, Boaz, you old charmer! I will be waiting by the phone for your call."

Natasha stepped over to where paramedics were still working on Kenneth, and looked down at him. "Are you going to live?" she asked.

"These idiots claim that the holes in me don't seem to have gone through anything important, and managed to go all the way through without leaving any lead inside me. If they're right, then I probably won't bleed to death internally, or die of lead poisoning anytime soon. Have you got us out of here?"

"Of course," she said. "Don't you know that I simply live to pull your ass out of the fires you get it into? I got you listed as three of my people, so that no matter what happened here today I could try to cover you. Seems it was a wise precaution."

"Yeah, I'd say so. How's Sam?"

She glanced over her shoulder, then looked back at Ken. "I haven't spoken directly to him yet, but he was keeping his wits about him. That's the most important thing, at this stage. Let's get them out of here, and we'll find out how he's holding up."

She hooked her head at him, and he pushed the paramedics away as he got to his feet. They walked back over to where Sam was still sitting in the chair he'd been in when Ben Yazdi was interrogating him. "Come on, Jim," Ken said. "The boss lady's here, and she says it's time to go back to work."

Sam nodded, and got to his feet. For once, he hadn't managed to get himself shot. The impacts that had knocked him down more than once had simply come from people trying to get out of the line of fire. He followed them out of the restaurant and down the street to where Natasha had parked her car.

When they got inside the vehicle, with Sam in the back seat and Kenneth in the front, Sam put a hand over his eyes. "The sons of bitches killed Harry," he said.

Natasha looked at him in the rearview mirror. "Harry knew what he was getting himself into," she said, "and we all know the risks involved in what we do. However," she pointed to the ear piece in her right ear, "I got word while I was still talking to Boaz that the old buzzard isn't dead. Apparently, taking a bullet through your right cheek is enough to send you into catatonic shock, so you can be forgiven for thinking he was dead. He also took one in the chest, punctured his right lung. They were going to rush him into surgery as soon as he got to the hospital."

Sam stared into the mirror at her eyes. "Lady, if you're lying to me to keep me on the team..."

"Relax, Sam," Ken said. "She's a genuine bitch, and she'd lie to you about almost anything, except whether a man on your team is alive or dead. If she says Harry's still kicking, then he is. And that's great, but the question I want an answer to is where the hell Chandler got off to." He looked meaningfully at Natasha.

She shrugged her shoulders as she drove. "Got nothing, so far," she said. "Some of our people tried to follow as he took off, but he was running scared. It's hard to keep surveillance on someone who's panicked. We know a few places he goes, so we'll be watching them. He'll turn up, his kind always do."

"Let's hope so," Ken said. "We're running out of time on this guy. His assassination plots are set to be triggered within the next few days—we can't let them happen. As far as we know, he has to give the order himself. If he's dead, he can't do that."

"What about underlings?" Natasha asked. "If he has a deputy, someone he trusts with his administrative control..."

"As far as we know, Chandler doesn't allow anyone to know what he's doing. The only reason we have the information we do is because one of his people has a conscience. He got it to Sam's wife, and don't ask how that came about, and she got it to us."

Sam, in the back seat, leaned forward so that he was almost between them. "Look, we have to get him. This isn't a game, and it's not a sport, where our team might come out ahead of his team. This is about saving lives, and lots of them. We're not just looking at the lives that

might be lost in his absolutely diabolical scheme, but
what about the lives that will be lost in the wars that
could result? This jackass is trying to set the Muslim
world against the Christian world. We're already on the
brink of war in that arena; it wouldn't take much more
than a firecracker to set it off. That's exactly what
Chandler is out to do, because it will bring everything
closer to where he wants it to be."

Ken turned in his seat so that he could look Sam in
the eye, and doing so made him wince. He had taken
three wounds that went all the way through, and while
they apparently didn't do any critical damage, they
definitely tore up some muscle tissue. Almost every
move he made for a while was going to hurt. "Sam, you
don't have to tell us, you're preaching to the choir. We
understand exactly what the problem is, what we're up
against. Unfortunately, unless you've got a crystal ball
stashed away, we don't have any way to identify his
location."

Sam leaned back in his seat, frustration evident in
his face and manner. He ran a hand over his face, and
then suddenly froze. He reached into his pocket and
took out his cell phone, but before he dialed he looked
into the rearview mirror again at Natasha. "Does
Jerusalem have traffic cameras? Video cameras, tied into
a network somewhere?"

She looked at him oddly in the mirror for a
moment, and then gave a curt nod. "Yes, but it's rather
secret. They installed regular traffic cameras on some

high risk traffic accident intersections and it raised a public outcry, claiming that the cameras were only designed to increase government revenues from fines. That's why, when they put in the video system, it was kept secret."

"Where is it run out of? What department?"

"The public safety department, but it's managed from an office in the building securities department, the department that oversees security in publicly accessible government buildings."

Sam dialed his phone, and waited for a moment as his call went halfway around the world. Indie answered a moment later. "Sam? Are you okay?"

"I'm fine, Baby," he said, "but we need your help. Can you and Herman get into the security network that takes care of public government buildings in Israel? They run it out of the Israeli Department of Public Safety, but it's handled through the office that takes care of building security, because it's a big secret that the government here spies on its citizens."

Indie hesitated, but only for a second. "We'll try. What are we looking for?"

"There's a little restaurant named Isaac's, it's just off of King George Street. Find it on the map, and then find all of the cameras closest to it. What you're looking for is a very frightened Chandler. He got away, and he's running for his life at the moment. We don't know where he's gone, so I'm hoping you can give us a lead."

"Okay. I got enough photos of him in this computer to let Herman's facial recognition programming do its job. He can scan a lot faster than I can. It will take us a little time to get into that network, but if there's a way, we'll do it. I'll call you soon as I got something. Love you!"

"Love you more! Call me soon as you can." He hung up the phone. "That's my wife, and she's probably the most brilliant computer hacker in the world. She wrote a program she calls Herman that seems to be able to get into just about any network, anywhere, and find whatever information we need. US Homeland Security is fully aware of her abilities, so forget about this as soon as I'm done telling you."

"Forget about what? I never heard a thing. Let's just hope your nonexistent wife and her nonexistent friend can do us some existent good. I'm listening to the chatter from my people, and it's not going very well. They lost him within half a block of the restaurant. Pretty bad, considering he was on foot and running like a maniac."

"Just because I'm curious," Ken said, "why the hell is it your people didn't just blow him away when he came running out of there?"

Natasha glanced at him, with a look of disgust in her eyes. "Kenneth, I'm on a short budget! Most of the people I use for surveillance jobs and such are college students and housewives, just people who need to earn a little extra money. They are not agents, and they are not killers."

Ken shook his head, and rolled his eyes. "No wonder things went to hell in Benghazi," he muttered. "And to think we used to be the most powerful nation on earth."

"Yeah, well, that was back when everyone else was more afraid of the Soviet Union's policies than they were of America's. What good is Sherlock Holmes, if he doesn't have Moriarty? Without the constant threat of Soviet communism hanging over the heads of every other nation on earth, none of them seem to feel that they need the great American watchdog, and so your country has lost a lot of respect. Add to this the fact that your last four presidents have weakened you in both foreign policy and your military, and all that greatness has gone down the toilet."

"Hey!" said Sam. "I'll have you know, that's my country you're talking about! Maybe you're right, and we're not as powerful as we used to be, but I can tell you right now that the United States of America is still the greatest country in the world. Yeah, it may have its problems, but it's still the best!"

Ken turned his head and looked at Sam. "You still think so? Our country is so messed up that the most evil terrorist ever born has been working right at the head of our national security. Now, he's loose on the world, and you and I are just about all there is that's available to try to stop him. You want to tell me what's so great about that?"

Sam smiled grimly. "Simple," he said, "it's because in any other country, there wouldn't be the two of us to go after the sonofabitch."

Ken stared at him for a moment, and then began to laugh. "Dear God, I'm saddled with an optimist. Sam, we may be down to hours left to find and stop this madman. Somehow, the two of us being the ones to do it isn't inspiring an awful lot of confidence."

"I'll make it even worse," Natasha said. "For all we know, Chandler may have given the orders to execute his plans even before he left Washington. Killing him may not stop them."

"She's got a good point," Sam said. "Maybe we should change our attack, try to take him alive. That way, we can at least try to get enough information out of him to put a stop to whatever is going on there, to whatever is already set into motion."

"Holy Jesus, Mary and Joseph," Ken said, his hands over his face. "Sam, do you have any clue how hard it's going to be just get close enough to kill him? Now multiply that times fifty, and you're looking at a pretty good picture of our chance of taking him alive."

Sam sat back in silence as Natasha drove, and when he got quiet, so did they. They rode the rest of the way back to the hotel without speaking, and once Natasha had parked the car the three of them walked in silence into the hotel and the elevator. Ken pushed the button for their floor.

"Three different people in the lobby made sure to watch us get into the elevator," Sam said.

"Of course," Natasha said. "Boaz is nothing if not efficient. Those would be his people, sent here to watch you, but not to interfere. Like any good policeman, he simply wants to know what's going on in his jurisdiction. Since I can't tell him the truth, he's going to try to find out in his own way."

The elevator opened, and they went to their room. Natasha followed, of course, then went straight to the bar once they got inside. "I need a drink," she said. "Anyone else?"

Ken raised a hand as he sat on the couch. "Make mine a double of whatever you're drinking."

"I don't drink," Sam said, and both of them stared at him.

Natasha shook her head. "You stay around Harry long enough, you will."

Sam looked up. "Speaking of Harry, any updates?"

Natasha grinned as she handed a glass to Ken. "Apparently he's in surgery now, and a nurse has told my people there that it's going very well, he's expected to survive with no major complications. You can probably be talking to him in a few hours, if you want."

Sam shook his head. "I don't want to talk to him. All he'd do is read me the riot act for letting Chandler get away. I'd much rather we have Chandler in custody somewhere by the time I talk to Harry."

He was still standing, so Sam wandered through the room and checked for any signs that it had been searched. He found a few things that looked slightly out of place, but he couldn't be certain that actually been moved. Everything they had brought with them was innocuous, and the only thing in the room that could connect them to weapons or clandestine activities was the empty salesman's case, the one Natasha had used to bring them their weapons. They hadn't left anything behind that could be incriminating, so he went back out front and sat down beside Ken.

"Both of you need to get some rest," Natasha said. "Sam, you're lucky enough not to have any holes in your body that God didn't put there, so you should go and get a shower, now. When you're finished, I can help Ken to get a bath, and clean his wounds, change his bandages. Then you should both get some sleep. I'll stay here tonight, so as soon as any word comes in, I'll let you know."

Sam nodded, and got back up from the couch. "A shower sounds good," he said. "I won't be long." He walked into the suite's bedroom and got a change of clothes from his bag, and was singing in the shower a few moments later, his voice carrying all through the suite.

If anybody had told me,
That someone like you,
Could ever love me,

The way that you do,
I'd've said, "You're a liar,
There's just two things I believe,
Only fools play with fire,
And there's no love for me."

Natasha looked at Ken. "Do you have to put up without all the time?"

"He sings with some band back home," he said. "I guess singing in the shower is how he rehearses."

She looked towards the bathroom door, and then shrugged. "Well, he isn't that bad. Beats listening to your snoring."

When Sam came out of the shower, Natasha helped Ken get to his feet and to the bathroom. She shut the door behind them, so Sam sat down and picked up the remote for the TV. Channel ten was running its news program, so he left it on and watched.

The announcer, a gray-haired man, smiled into the camera as he spoke. "... And the Russian president says that there will be severe implications for the country's relationship with Turkey after this incident."

Sam watched the program for about fifteen minutes, keeping an eye on the scrolling ticker that rolled along the bottom of the screen. All of the news headlines for the day appeared there, but the only mention of the shootings at the restaurant was a brief comment by the announcer that what appeared to be a random shooting had occurred. He stressed that the government had found no connection to any terrorist activity or group, and that Israel police were investigating.

Sam shook his head, and began flipping channels. He found the government-sponsored channels, as well as those that were designed primarily for tourists, such as the Western Wall channel and others. There were a couple of channels devoted strictly to music, both American and Israeli, and he listened for a few seconds to each of them before moving on.

He found a movie, one he thought he'd seen before but couldn't remember for sure, and just left it on to create some background noise. It gave him the opportunity to tune out for a bit, and relax. After a couple of minutes, he stretched out on the couch, tucking one of its pillows under his head.

With everything that had happened, Sam didn't believe he'd be able to go to sleep, so he was startled when his telephone rang and it woke him from a dream of being at home with Indie and Kenzie. He sat up quickly and grabbed the phone from the end table.

"Hello?"

"Sam? Babe, it's me," Indie said. "I think I got you something."

"Baby, that would be great. What is it?"

"Okay," she said, "if you get on Hebron Road, and go south a few miles, you'll come to Asher Viner Street, going off to the east. It's like an exit there, take it and follow the road to the east about a mile, you'll pass a bunch of fields on the right, like farm fields. That will bring you to a circle, take it out to the Northeast, and you'll come to another one in like a quarter mile or so. If you turn right there, you'll be on Moshe Barazani Street. He turned in at the third drive on the right about an hour ago, and went inside. As far as I can tell, he hasn't come back out."

Sam smiled and the phone. "Baby, how on earth did you manage this?"

"Well, like I told you, I had enough pictures of him that Herman could start a facial recognition search. It paid off, because he spotted Chandler on foot by King George Street, but I guess he had called someone because a moment after that, the camera got him getting into a car. Herman just kept scanning, though, and kept spotting his face at different intersections. By scanning all of the cameras along a particular route, he could keep looking for him and get an idea of where he might turn up next. When he turned off onto Moshe whatever street, it just happened that the camera could see the house where he parked. We saw them get out of the car and go in, and I've been watching that camera, but he doesn't seem to have come back out. Of course, I can't see the back of the house, so I can't be sure he's still there."

"Indie, baby, you're as awesome and wonderful as ever," Sam said, "and I'm even starting to like Herman a little bit. This is incredible, and might be exactly what we needed. If you see anything change, please let me know immediately. I love you!"

"I love you, too. I'll call you if anything changes at all." She hung up, and Sam looked at the time. It was almost midnight, but he didn't feel that they could wait until morning. He called out for Ken, and he and Natasha came out of the bedroom a moment later.

He quickly filled them in on Indie's call, and Natasha shook her head. "And how is it we haven't already recruited this girl?"

"Sam beat us to it, he married her," Ken said. "Seems that she's part of the package deal we get when Harry calls on Sam, though, so that helps. She's definitely a whiz at this stuff, I've seen a bit of her in action before."

"Fine, okay, whatever," Natasha said. "Just as long as she's on our side, that's all I care about at this moment." She had reached into her big purse and produced a tablet computer, on which she was calling up a map of the area Indie had described. "The third driveway," she mused. "Oh, this is not good. That is the home of an attaché from the Libyan Embassy. I know her, and frankly, it would surprise me if she were knowingly involved in any of Chandler's plans. She's not a militant, not in any way."

Ken scowled. "Are you saying that this woman has diplomatic immunity? That we'd be invading Libyan soil if we go in there after him?"

Natasha was nodding her head. "That's exactly what

I'm saying," she said. "As far as any government is concerned, that house is in Libya. Any entry that is uninvited can be construed as an act of war."

"Well, you said you know her. Can you get us an invitation?" Sam asked. "I mean, as far as we know, Chandler doesn't know you're involved, right?"

Natasha gave him a look that could have peeled paint off his Corvette. "And I'd very much like to keep it that way," she said. "I'm off the reservation on this, working only as a favor to Harry Winslow. If my superiors find out what I'm doing, it could mean my job, possibly even my freedom."

"Natasha, come on," Ken said. "When have you ever worried about what your superiors might think? And as for your job or your freedom, you know too many secrets for anyone to seriously pose a risk to either one. Now, can you get us in there, or not?"

"To be honest, I would doubt it. If she's involved, she's going to probably refuse, and at the very least she would let him know that someone was coming. Even if we got in, he'd be ready for us, and then there's that whole war on foreign soil thing."

Sam shook his head. "I don't care," he said. "We have got to capture this guy, and find out somehow whether he's got his plans already set in motion, or if he's got someone ready to give the orders. We have to stop the things he's up to, no matter what it takes."

25

2

"You cannot stay here," Yusrah said. "If what you say is true, then your own countrymen are trying to kill you. I cannot risk involving the embassy or any of my family or staff, here, in your troubles. You have to go, now."

"Yusrah, don't even think about trying to turn your back on me now," Chandler said to her. "You owe me far too much, and I will collect on that debt. Remember that you would not have your position, were it not for me. I can remove you just as quickly as I installed you, and before you consider any plan to eliminate me, remember that I have people who know where I am even now. Should anything happen to me, their orders are to make certain that retaliation finds its way back to you. Any questions?"

"Mr. Chandler, this is not about failure to pay my debt. It is about keeping what is between us in the secret level where it must remain. In that, I have no choice, for if it becomes too widely known, then we will both be endangered." The attaché seemed to think over her options. "It is also not about whether I fear you or not. I will do all I can to help you, as I have agreed, but I can be no help to you if I am exposed and removed from my place."

Chandler grinned at her. "Well, at this moment, we are both safer with me sitting right here. No one can touch me within your home, and it will give me a chance to find out just what is going on behind the scenes. I have absolutely no interest in walking into a trap when I leave here, so you're just going to have to put up with me for now. And incidentally, I'm hungry. My afternoon has not gone well, as you know, and I could use something to eat."

Yusrah inclined her head in submission. "Feeding you will not be a problem," she said. "I have an excellent kitchen staff, away from some of the finest restaurants in all of Israel. I shall order for you a full dinner." She rose from her chair and started out of the room.

Chandler caught her hand as she passed him. "Yusrah, don't make the mistake of trying to betray me while you're out of my sight. Remember, I never bluff. If I tell you that retaliation will find you, you can count on it."

She looked down at him. "I have no intention of betraying you," she said. "I am only going to the kitchen to arrange your dinner. Are you becoming paranoid, Mr. Chandler? I can imagine that having your own men attempting to murder you could cause you to see the dangers around every corner, but you can relax. You are not in danger here, not from me or my people. Not only do I owe you a great debt, but my country also owes you. The position you have offered us in the order that is to come is one that we could not have expected under other circumstances. I am not one to bite the hand that feeds me, Mr. Chandler, and my country is not one to forget to whom it should be grateful. Now, if you will excuse me?"

He let go of her hand, and she smiled as she proceeded out of the room. Chandler glanced over at Yusuf, the driver who had picked him up and brought him here. "Go with her—make sure that arranging dinner is all she's up to."

Yusuf smiled, and rose to follow Yusrah. It was obvious from his demeanor that he enjoyed following her down the hall. Chandler admitted to himself that she was an attractive woman. He wouldn't mind a dalliance with her, and he knew that he could have it with the snap of his fingers. However, he hated to become romantically involved with a woman he was likely to have to kill. It left such an ugly taste behind, killing someone you've made love to.

He reached into a pocket and took out a clean phone, then dialed the number for Gary Stone back in the states. It took three rings for Gary to answer.

"Hello?" The computer nerd said.

"It's me," Chandler said, counting on Gary's recognition of his voice to be all the identification he would need. "Things have gone crazy over here. Have you heard anything about any official sanctions against me?"

Gary had prepared himself for the question, knowing it would be coming at some point before the day was over. "No, sir, I haven't heard anything like that. Is there something wrong?"

"You're damned right something's wrong," Chandler said. "I sat down at my scheduled meeting a few hours ago, and was almost killed by a death squad attack, some of our people. I got away, but I lost some good men and I'm pretty damned pissed. I want you to dig into everything you can find, and see who's behind them. I recognized all three—they were Kenneth Long, Harry Winslow and that man of his, Sam Prichard. I think Winslow was killed, Long was wounded but may still be alive, I'm not sure about Prichard. Find out for me and get back to me on this number. And Gary, don't waste any time!"

Gary nodded into the phone, just as if he were being sincere. "Yes, sir, I'm on it. I'll get back to you as soon as possible." He ended the call instantly, the way he always did.

While Chandler was waiting for his dinner, late as it was, Gary was just about to have his own a little earlier than usual. He had microwaved a chimichanga, poured himself a glass of orange juice and was just about to chow down when Chandler had called. After he hung up, he looked down at his food and pushed it away. Something about talking to Chandler just ruined his appetite.

Gary had barely had any sleep since meeting with those two men a couple nights before. He had finally begun to relax that afternoon, mostly because he hadn't heard from Chandler and had allowed himself to hold that those men have done what they had planned to do, which was eliminate Gary's boss from the face of the earth. That phone call told Gary that things had not gone according to their plans, and that was going to make it much more difficult for them to accomplish their mission.

Gary had read through Chandler's notes a half-dozen times, and he was literally terrified of what would happen if those men failed. Chandler had to be stopped, but Gary didn't know what he could do to stop the sonofabitch. He was just a programmer, a hacker, he'd never had any training with weapons or strategies. There was not really anything he could do, other than the offer what clandestine support he could to those who were trying to do what was right.

Absently, he picked up the orange juice and took a sip, then thought over the day back at his office. He knew that a lot of the muscle there was extremely loyal to Chandler, so there was no hope of recruiting anyone from inside that part of the organization to help him deal with the problem. He passed them over without a second's thought, and then began looking at all of the rest of the staff of the senior Muslim desk. He poked through all of their computer terminals, scanned all of their emails, tapped all of their phones and read through their text messages — only one person, a girl in the analytics office, even seemed to be aware that Chandler was going off the deep end, and her attitude was one of, "What I don't know, or pretend not to know, probably won't hurt me too badly." That was the way most people would respond, by sticking their heads in the sand like a bunch of ostriches. Far be it from the human animal, other than a few spectacular examples, to want to stand up against the threat to all of his fellows. Most people were simply cowards, only concerned about self-preservation. In Gary's opinion, those were the ones least worthy of any preservation whatsoever.

But then, there were those spectacular individuals, the ones who stood out in a crowd because they would never just sit back and shut up. These were the ones who would fight against all odds for what they knew was the right thing to do, regardless of how it might look to everyone else, regardless of how the law might see it. They were the ones who accepted the responsibility for the safety of the rest of their race, and Gary Stone had met a pair of them just a couple nights before. He had honestly put a star on his kitchen calendar to mark the day.

On the other hand, they weren't the only two he had

met that day. There was another one, one whose face he had not seen, but whom he knew even better than those he'd met in person. He went to his computer, ran all the scans to make sure no one was tapping into it or watching what he was doing, disabled the keystroke loggers that were required by his security clearance and which supposedly could not be disabled, and then sent a message.

Stony: Herman, are you there?

He waited for about three minutes, and then the response appeared on the screen.

Herman: I'm here. What's up?

Stony: just heard from the boss. Sounds like your boys didn't do too well. Got a sit rep on them?

Herman: just sent them some Intel a little while ago. I know things went bad, but not how bad. Any news on them from your end?

Stony: I hear one may be dead, another wounded, no word on your guy, though, sorry.

Herman: my guy is okay. He didn't say anything about fatalities or wounds, so don't know.

Stony: Herman, my boss is crazy.

Herman: you want to tell me something I don't know?

Stony: look, I got nobody my end I can trust, and I mean nobody. If he finds out I'm talking to you, no one will ever find my body. That's the world I live in. But right now, I know it's my time to decide which side I'm on, and I only got two choices, him or you. If I choose him, I'll be worse than Hitler's top man, but if I choose you, I will probably end up dead and not very far off. Then again, I never expected to live forever, but I do want to be able to look in the mirror while I am alive. Guess that means I got no real choice, I choose you. Tell me how I can help?

Herman: keep doing what you're doing. Get us everything you can on him and on his plans. I know they're worried about whether someone is ready to make his plans happen if he falls. Who is back up? Is there a backup?

Stony: there is one, don't know who. I'll see what I can find out, but don't hold your breath waiting for me. Keep the channel open. I'll get back to you as soon as I can, and hopefully I'll find something worthwhile. Tell your guy I'm on it, and if they've got anybody who could cover my back, I'd appreciate it.

Herman: will do. Good luck.

Gary sat back and looked at the computer, and a strange sense of accomplishment went through him. He had come to that point that every man reaches sooner or later, the point where he has to decide where he stands, and he had made the decision that felt right to him. He knew what the consequences most likely would be, but he had made the decision that he couldn't live with the alternative, so he stood on what he believed. Gary was proud of himself, more proud than he had ever been.

So, he thought, *they need to find out who Mr. Chandler's backup man could be. All I've seen in the notes are references to "M," who seems to be the one to take over if anything happens to the boss.* He ran through all of the people he could think of whose last names began with M, but he didn't know of any who might conceivably fit the bill for the backup man or woman.

He opened Mad Maggie, his own special hacking program. He fed into it every connection he could find to Chandler, every relative, everyone who owed him favors, every person who served on the committee that oversaw his activities, and instructed the program to look for anything about any of them or anyone connected to them that might make them a likely candidate for M. When he had the program ready to go, he hesitated with his finger over the execute button, reminding himself that once he executed the search, there would be no going back. This was the point at which he truly made his commitment to his choice, and for a brief few seconds, he seriously considered changing his mind and letting Chandler find out about the men he had helped.

He looked at the execute button, and smiled. "Oh, what the hell! This is bound to be a lot more fun!" His finger stabbed the button, and Gary Stone became a man.

Back in Jerusalem, Chandler was wolfing down the

unusual meal of fish, rice and spices that have been set in front of him, and finding it quite enjoyable. He was sitting up close to Yusrah's desk, using it for a table. She sat on the other side, watching him with interest.

"You eat as if you believe there won't be any food left for you when this is gone," she said.

"Something like that," he replied. "The way things are, I don't know for sure when I'll get another chance to have a meal, so I'm going to eat as much as I can right now without slowing myself down. That's a survival tactic, one we learned in the field. Eat when you can, rest when you can, for there is no way to predict when you will get another opportunity."

"Oh, I quite understand the philosophy," she said. "Believe it or not, I was not always a desk jockey. Isn't that what you Americans call a diplomat? Someone who rides a desk all day?"

Chandler shrugged his shoulders. "That would be one of many derogatory terms we use," he said. "There are lots of others, but I never cared for that type of tomfoolery. If I have something to say about someone, or about how they do their jobs, I prefer to say it to their faces. It's so much more satisfying to see the look in their eyes when they realize what I can do to them."

"I know precisely what you can do to me," Yusrah said. "You do not frighten me, Mr. Chandler. I resigned myself to the type of death I will suffer long ago, and frankly I have lived long past the time when I expected it to claim me. I do not aid you because I fear you, I aid you because I desire the rewards you have offered me. The same is true of my country. Can we therefore dispense with talk of threats and retaliations, and discuss what help you may need from me at this time."

Chandler looked at her as he chewed his latest mouthful, and then shrugged. "Fair enough," he said. "I have three men I need to meet with in the morning, so I need secure transportation to the café down the street from the French Embassy. That's where we are meeting, and of course I want that kept under the tightest secrecy. I got lucky today—I can't count on being that lucky if they catch up with me again. Oh, and I'll need weapons. I had to ditch mine, and Yusuf has only a handgun. I do not wish to be caught unprepared again."

Yusrah nodded. "We have weapons, and I can have one of my drivers take you to your meeting. Now, the question then is, will you be returning here? As I've said, that is not a comfortable position for me or for my country. You need to find another place to stay."

"I won't need to come back, not tomorrow. The men I'm meeting will have new accommodations arranged, so I'll thank you for your hospitality and move along. However, remember that I will need you next week, when everything goes into motion. Your outcry must be loud and unmistakable; you are ready, aren't you?"

"Of course we are ready," she said, and he could

hear the frustration in her voice. "Remember, Mr. Chandler, the things that you are doing will result in the deaths of many of my countrymen. Even more, it will mean deaths for those who share the Muslim faith throughout the world. The sacrifices are necessary, we agree, but that does not mean that we take them lightly. On the contrary, we take these sacrifices and our responsibilities quite seriously, and expect of you to do the same. These are the lives of my brothers and cousins that are being spilled upon your battleground. They must not be wasted."

"On that we agree," Chandler said. "None of what we're doing can be wasted, none of it can be ineffective. This plan has been laid for thousands of years, and is only now coming into its time. Shamash has waited a long, long time for someone to bring his prophecies into reality. These prophecies were made almost five thousand years ago, more than twenty five hundred years before the birth of Christ. They foretell this age, when the societies of the earth are becoming more and more corrupt and evil, so that they're heading towards what can only be their own ultimate destruction. If Shamash allowed it to continue much longer, there would be no world left for his people to rule. I am fortunate to have been chosen, and everyone who helps me will be rewarded. This really is an incredible opportunity."

"But it comes at a price," Yusrah said. "The rest of the world will see you only as a monster, and the Christians will call you the Devil, or worse."

"So what? They won't even know who I am. I'm not a fool, you know; there are those who are well suited to being out in the public eye, and then there are those who can make the plans and decisions that are necessary in order to properly rule something as large as a whole world. That's me. I've got people in place to be the ones out front, the ones who point the fingers of blame where I want them pointed, and then offer the answers that the world needs in order to survive. Let the world think what it wants to, as long as they obey and do as they're told."

Yusrah rose once again and walked out of the room. Chandler watched her go, and like Yusuf, he admired the view. There was no doubt that she was an attractive woman, and had kept herself in shape. Women weren't his concern right now, however, because there were much more important matters he needed to attend to.

First, he needed to deal with the problem of these two rogue agents who were trying to gun him down. While he might actually understand their reluctance to allow his plans to go through, he could not allow them to succeed in their attempts to stop him. It was just too important that he accomplish the things Shamash had set before him.

Chandler often wondered how it was that so many religious scholars failed to see that Shamash must be the true God over all. All of the other religions, he was convinced, had merely copied so much of what Shamash had done, so many of his prophecies and predictions. Was it so difficult to see what was right before your eyes?

38

Apparently, for some, it was.

Chandler finished eating and got up to leave the office. He had already been assigned a room, and it was getting quite late, so he decided to go and get some rest. Yusrah would take care of the details for the morning, so he could relax, at least for a little while. He followed the hallway to get to his room, and sat down on the bed to take off his shoes. He was incredibly tired, and could feel himself trying to doze off even as he lay back on the bed.

* * * * *

"We can't sit back and do nothing," Sam said. "As it stands right now, we don't know what he's up to, where he's going – we've got no intel!"

Sam's phone rang, and he snatched it up. It was Indie calling again, and he answered quickly. "Hey, baby, what you got?"

"I just talked to that computer guy a little bit ago, and he's working on trying to get you some kind of information. I told him that I thought one of the things you're concerned about is who Chandler might have ready to take his place, if anything happens to him. Is that right?"

"Yeah, it is. In fact, that's sort of the big issue, right at the moment. We're trying to decide whether we should just eliminate him, or try to take him alive so that we can hopefully get that information out of him."

Indie was quiet for a moment, and Sam knew she

was wrestling with the knowledge that he was talking about killing Chandler, about cold blooded murder. Sure, she knew it was necessary, but that didn't make it easier to handle. "So, if this guy could get you that information, then there's a possibility you wouldn't have to expose yourselves to so much risk, am I right?"

"That about sums it up," Sam said. "The other problem we've got is that that place you located belongs to another country's diplomatic mission. We can't do anything there, nothing at all. If we had any way to know when he might be leaving, or where he might be going when he does, that might give us a better chance of success. If you happen to talk to your friend again, ask him about whether he could get us that information."

"All right, I'll get ahold of him and see if he has any ideas on that line. Other than that, how are you doing, Sam?"

Sam looked at Natasha and Ken, and shrugged his shoulders. Natasha had her own phone out, and was whispering furiously into it. "Baby, I wish I'd never heard of any of this," he said. "I wish I was back home in our house, with you and Kenzie, and didn't even have any clue these things were going on. Trouble is, I do know, and I can't sit back and hope that someone else can deal with it. That's just not my way."

He heard Indie hold back a sniffle. "I know that, Sam," she said, "and it's part of why I love you so much.

Okay, so let me get this straight. You need any information you can get on where and when Chandler might be going from where he's at now, as well as any info on who he might have as his second-in-command, or backup person. Am I missing anything?"

"Not that I can think of. I guess the big issue, right now, is whether taking him down is going to be enough to stop his plans. If we knew that for sure, it could make a world of difference. As long as we're not certain of that point, then we could just be making things worse."

Indie gave a sarcastic laugh. "Well, then maybe it's a good thing that you haven't had greater success before now, right?"

Sam smiled. "Yeah, I guess that's right. Thanks for rubbing my nose in it." He closed his eyes and thought for a moment, then opened them again. "Something else," he said. "Ask your buddy if he can get us anything on the people Chandler might have working with him from other countries. That could be critical, and the first one he could be looking at is the woman who lives in that house where he's hiding right now. She's some sort of helper in the Libyan mission; ask him to find out anything he can on how she might be involved, or her government."

Indie said she'd get hold of Gary right away, told Sam she loved him and hung up. He looked at Ken and Natasha, who were sitting there watching him as if hoping he was about to pull a miracle out of his ass. He shrugged and smiled.

"Well, she's trying to get us some serious intel, so that we know what we're up against. She's got somebody in Chandler's office who's willing to feed her information, and beggars can't be choosers. We need whatever we can get, as far as intelligence. Keep your fingers crossed that she does us some good."

Natasha shook her head in irony. "Ken," she said. "If someone had told me a week ago that today I would be sitting here with a rogue agent and an ex-cop turned private eye whose wife does better cyber work than the entire cyber warfare division of the company, and that the fate of most of the free world probably depends on what our little band can do, I would have refused to believe it. And if whoever it was managed to convince me that it was true, I would probably have gone into my bedroom and blown out my own brains."

Kenneth Long burst out laughing, and it took him a moment to get himself back under control. "Natasha, you would've done no such thing. Just the absolute incongruity of the whole concept would have been enough to make sure you would stick around just to see what might happen."

She looked at him for a moment, then shrugged and rolled her eyes. "You're probably right," she said, "but that doesn't mean that I wouldn't have been smarter to blow my own brains out. Let's face it, we don't exactly have a lot of hope, here. I mean, come on, there's a pretty good chance we're about to see the entire world turned on its ear. Boys, if we don't stop him, this insane plan of his to turn so much of the world against itself is probably gonna work! You take all of these countries and pit them against each other, you're going to have chaos. Now, if somebody steps up who can get enough of their attention long enough to make them listen to a plan that could bring clarity to it all, then you got yourself a new world leader. I don't know about you guys, but that scares the hell out of me!"

Sam grinned. "Not long ago, I would have agreed with you completely. The thing is, I just had an incredible crash course in prophecy, and as far as I can tell, there's still a very, very slim chance that Chandler really is a part of what's supposed to be happening, even if we disagree, he and I, on which prophecies to believe. Now, I think he's a fake, and that he's simply trying to take power for himself that is not intended to be his. If he's not real, then he's nothing but a terrorist, a monster, and a monster needs to be put down. Holy crap, haven't you guys ever watched *Supernatural?* Monsters have to die, just ask Sam and Dean!"

"Well, there's not much doubt he's a monster," Ken said. "I guess the only real question remaining is what we have to use against him. Silver bullets? Wooden stakes? What's it going to take?"

"Sam and Dean – and incidentally, that's one of my favorite American television programs – those two never had to deal with anything as evil and real as Grayson

Chandler. Somehow I doubt that even with all the information they had on monsters and such,that they could have found a reference to the special, magical weapon that is necessary to deal with one like this guy. I don't think we need silver, I think plain old lead will do it; however, I'll confess that I'm beginning to think we need to sanctify it with prayers and maybe some holy water!"

Sam leaned forward and buried his face in his hands again. "Look, if we can't touch him where he's at, then we've got a mess on our hands, already. Natasha, can you put someone out there to watch, see when he leaves and which way he's going?"

"Already done," she said. "I took care of that while you were on the phone with your wife again. I'll have three people watching him from three different angles within twenty minutes. If and when he moves, we'll know it."

Sam nodded. "Kinda figured that's what you were doing, good job. So, I guess the only thing for us to do right now is to try to get some rest. Natasha, just be sure to wake us if you get any word. Now, get off my couch, I want to try to snooze as much as I can between now and whenever all hell breaks loose. Next time we get Chandler in our sights, I don't want his luck holding out any longer. I don't care how many false gods he's got on his side, I want the son of a bitch's throat in my grasp, and I want his balls where I can crush them if that's what it takes to break him."

Natasha grinned, then took Ken's hand and led him back to the bedroom. He didn't put up any resistance, Sam noticed, although it was doubtful he was capable of much more than resting. Something about bullet wounds had a tendency to eliminate thoughts of any other activities, unless those activities were necessary to survival.

Sam moved back to the couch and adjusted the pillow, then lay down and tried to relax.

3

Herman: Stony, are you around?

Gary Stone saw the message appear in a box on the right of his screen.

Stony: I'm working. What's up?

Herman: talked to my guy. We know where your boss is, but he's untouchable as long as he's there.

Stony: yeah, DI. If they do anything there, could trigger WW3.

Herman: bingo. Can you get anything on when he might move and where to?

Gary didn't type anything for a couple of moments, and Indie knew he was probably thinking it over. A moment later, she saw the little icon that indicated he was typing.

Stony: don't know anything yet. If I were to call him and say I had some way to know your guys were going to move on him, he'd probably head out fast, but I wouldn't know where to. We might use that as a last resort, make him jump out in front of them, right? Meanwhile, I'll try to figure his next move while Maggie is working on identifying his Number Two.

Herman: Maggie?

Stony: lol. My version of your Herman. Maybe someday we can introduce them, let them play chess.

Herman: introduce a pair of AI programs to each other? Scary. Suppose they hit it off and give birth to something that decides people are no longer necessary?

Stony: Good point, I'd hate to be grandpa to the Terminator or something worse.

Herman: yeah. Bad enough we got your boss. The things he's out to do would be just as bad for humanity as Skynet.

Stony: all too true. Okay, let me get back to it. If I get anything, I'll let you know.

Gary sat there and stared at his laptop's screen. He wasn't sure exactly who Indie was, but she had guts, he was sure of that. She had to know that her computer could be traced when she was talking to him, and for all she knew, he could be playing her, stringing her along to keep her and her husband guessing about what Chandler knew or didn't know.

He reached for the keyboard again, and began entering information into Maggie. One of her built-in functions was to scan all the computers in the offices that

Gary worked in, and he told the program that he wanted rapid notification of any internal messaging through the system, from or to Chandler. When he had finished giving the program these instructions, he started looking over the results he had been getting from his previous search.

Like Indie's Herman, Mad Maggie displayed results in a list of links to other files, whether on Gary's own computer, somewhere in the network from the office or even on the web. The first page of results showed literally dozens of links, and he began scanning through them.

The first twenty all seemed to be of people connected to Chandler through his personal life. Gary had told Maggie to look for anything that might connect particular individuals to the "M" that kept turning up in Chandler's notes, and she had done her job. Maggie had searched through all of Chandler's notes about people he knew, looking for any "M" notation, and had found several. Unfortunately, he had forgotten to tell her to ignore a capital M that was part of a name or word, and to look only for instances where it appeared alone. He rolled his eyes and began re-writing his instructions, then turned the program loose once again.

That took only a few minutes, and then he was surprised to see that Maggie had already flagged some of Chandler's internal messages for his review. He popped open the page and looked them over.

The first message on the page seemed to be from Chandler to some unidentified woman in the international transactions office, asking her to forward to him a copy of a report she had done on Yusrah Almagia, a senior attaché in the business bureau of the Libyan Embassy to Israel in Jerusalem. The report had to do with transactions made between Libyan businesses and some companies in Europe, companies that kept turning up over and over in Chandler's notes. Klockenbrink Electronics, Fuhrler Engineering, Burkschwitz and Meierminsk, a law firm, and many others all had sent substantial sums of money to various companies in Spain, Austria, Italy and Great Britain, each of which was apparently approved by Ms. Almagia. Gary made a list of the transactions and added the companies behind them to Maggie's search parameters. The program would look up each company's officers and major stockholders to see if any of them might fit the profile he was building on "M."

The next message appeared to be from someone, possibly an analyst, over at the Russia desk. It said that Stas Nicklovitch, who was one of Russia's most brilliant biologists, had perfected a strain of wheat that was almost gluten free, would grow to harvest in eleven days and actually added nutrients to the soil. This feature allowed it to be replanted within a day of harvest, and it would grow well even in temperatures as low as the mid forties. This would allow it to produce as many as twenty five full crops per year in most climates, and sometimes more.

This announcement had been suppressed, the message said, in accordance with Chandler's instructions, and no news of the development had been allowed out of Nicklovitch's laboratory farms. Unfortunately, this had required the elimination of two of his assistants, Sabina Petrov and Yevgeni Utkin, who had tried to leak the information to WikiLeaks. Professor Nicklovitch was very upset about their deaths, but said that he understood the necessity, since the announcement of such a potent food source would mean the chance for many third world and less-developed nations to begin to feed their starving populations in ways that they had not been able to do previously.

Gary sat back in utter shock and stared at the monitor. A discovery of this nature could conceivably mean an end to world starvation; for Chandler to withhold it until he could have it announced to support his plans for world domination was to allow thousands, maybe millions, to starve to death when it wasn't necessary. He forced himself to accept the reality of what he was seeing, and went on.

The next few messages were simple and innocuous, having to do with staff members asking for time off, others wishing Chandler a happy birthday – Gary hadn't even known it was coming up – and other such things, so he skimmed through them quickly and went on.

The one after those, however, brought him up short. It was a terse message from an unidentifiable agent of Chandler's in Rome.

Thought you'd like to know that another Cardinal has come on board with us. That makes eight of the most prominent Cardinals, and gives us a solid majority in the College of Cardinals since so many of the others will follow their leads. The only holdout among the ones you wanted locked in is George Cardinal Simmons from Boston. He's here, right at the moment. Should I take any action on him?

Chandler was trying to manipulate the College of Cardinals? But why? The current Pope was in good health, so there wouldn't be a Conclave anytime soon – unless, of course, something unexpected should happen to the pope!

"Great God in Heaven," Gary whispered to himself, "he's going to have the pope assassinated!"

* * * * *

"He's moving!" Natasha said loudly, and Sam was up in an instant. "I just got the message, he's left Almagia's house and is heading this direction. Let's get out of this room, we're sitting ducks here!"

Ken was on his feet and slamming another pistol under his jacket, so Sam grabbed one and did the same. He took one of the Glocks that Natasha had brought them the day before, then snatched up a couple of the extra magazines. Natasha took the remaining nine mil, and they headed out the door toward the elevator.

"How could he know where we are?" Sam asked. "Did anyone in our office know?"

"No one," Natasha said. "At this moment, I'm wondering about the man your wife has been talking to. Perhaps she let our location slip, and he passed it along?"

Sam shook his head angrily. "She wouldn't make that mistake," he said. "Believe me, she's smarter than all of us put together, and her instincts are excellent. She'd never give him any information he could use against us."

"Well, if he's coming for us, then somebody did," she snapped back at him. "My watchers say that he's just turning onto King David Street, coming from the south. If he's coming to the hotel, he'll be here in two minutes."

"Then he'll find us waiting for him, in the lobby," Ken said. "There's no point in worrying, we've simply got to be ready for whatever may happen."

"Who's worried?" Natasha asked. "I never worry, I simply like to be prepared. I've found that it tends to keep me alive. Anything wrong with that?"

The elevator opened, and they stepped into the lobby. A quick look around told all three of them that there was nothing unusual in sight, so they spread out and walked in different directions, instinctively posting themselves where they could all watch the front door, but keep an eye on other entrances, as well. A couple of minutes passed, with no surprises, so Sam looked over at Natasha.

She was looking back in his direction, and hooked her head to tell him to come her way. He quickly stepped across the intervening space, and joined her just as Ken did.

"Surveillance says he turned on to Paul Emile Botta Street," she said. "He's apparently meeting someone for breakfast at Shlomo's. It's a popular place—indoors, quiet, secure; I doubt we could get in close enough to see him without being spotted."

"Great," Sam growled. Another chance we can't do anything with. Let's get down there and try to catch him as he's leaving, maybe we can at least follow him to somewhere we can try to take him."

Natasha rolled her eyes as if frustrated. "Okay, then let's go. We can follow, maybe, but remember that we're still looking at risk, here. If we take him down and he has someone waiting in the wings, we're back to square one, except we don't know who we're looking for. We can't risk that, Sam."

Sam smiled. "Who said anything about taking him down? I want to take him *in*, as in capture the sonofabitch! You let me have him for an hour, we'll know who his backup is."

Ken put a hand on his shoulder. "You can't count on that, Sam. Chandler is a religious fanatic, even if his religion is something so out there that none of us can understand it. I've seen religious fanatics withstand tortures that would crack anyone else."

"Well, we'll never know if we just stand around here talking about it, for God's sake, let's go!" Sam stormed away from them and headed for the door.

Ken looked at Natasha and shrugged. "He gets this way, sometimes. I think we better follow him, don't you?"

She laughed. "If we don't, God only knows what kind of mess we'll have to clean up. Let's go." The two of them followed Sam out the door and towards the parking lot.

Sam hadn't gotten that far ahead of them, and even with Ken limping a bit, they caught up with him before he got to her car. He glanced at each of them.

"Glad to see you decided to join the party," he said.

"Wouldn't miss it," said Ken. "I hear tell it could turn out to be quite a blast."

"That's what I'm hoping for," Sam said with a grin. "In fact, I'm counting on it."

They climbed into the car and Natasha got behind the wheel. She started up and backed out of the parking space without a word, then turned on to King David Street and headed for the intersection, already signaling her turn. The light was green when she got there, so she made the turn with no problem. Just a couple of blocks later, she pulled over to the side of the road and parked.

She pointed across the street at what appeared to be a small but fairly nice office building. "That's Shlomo's," she said. "The big building a couple doors down is the French Embassy, and there are those who think Shlomo's is simply a part of their mission. I think more

Embassy business gets done in Shlomo's than it ever does in their offices. Odds on, Chandler is meeting with French Embassy staff right now."

Ken nodded. "It's even worse than that," he said. "I bet you the sonofabitch is in there eating breakfast. You know what I'd give for a big plate of pancakes right now? Or French toast?"

"Shut up, you're making me hungry," Natasha said. "We don't have time to worry about food right now. That was always part of your problem, Kenneth, you always let inconsequential things distract you when there are more important matters to attend to."

"There is nothing more important than breakfast—it's the most important meal of the day! Didn't anyone ever teach you that? Oh, wait, I forgot. You're Russian, for you would be lunch that's most important, right?"

"Would you two grow up?" Sam asked. "Natasha, where are your surveillance people? Are you still in touch with them?"

"We did grow up, and we didn't like it, so we went back to acting like children just to annoy you. Yes, they're inside, still keeping an eye on Chandler. I've got a couple on him right now, a man and a woman. They don't look out of place in there, so he probably hasn't noticed them at all. I instructed them to let us know the moment he starts to leave."

"Good. Then I guess all we can do is wait." Sam leaned back in the backseat of the car and tried to relax.

"If I doze off, wake me when the fun starts. I'm for snatching the sonofabitch right now, if we can. Only question then is where we take him."

"If you figure out a way to grab him, I can handle that part," said Natasha. "There are still places around here where you can do that type of thing. You snatch him, and I'll show you where."

"Sounds good," Sam said. "Like I said, wake me up if things start happening."

The three of them relaxed and waited, with Ken and Natasha keeping an eye on the restaurant. A half hour passed, and then an hour. Sam actually managed to doze off for a bit, but the other two sat there wide awake the whole time. They played a game of tic-tac-toe on scrap paper to occupy themselves.

Suddenly, Natasha's eyes lit up. "He's up," she said, "and headed for the door. Apparently he's leaving with whoever it is he met with here. They'll be coming out the door in a second, there are six of them."

Sam sat up and looked toward the door. "Six of them?" he asked. "Do we have any idea how many might be armed?"

"If they're French Embassy, Sam, you can assume they all are. They're almost certainly DGSE, *Direction générale de la sécurité extérieure.* They're sort of like the CIA, though a bit more inclined to be public about their affairs. Duck down, here they come."

* * * * *

56

It was after midnight, but Indie couldn't sleep. She was sitting on the bed, computer in her lap and Kenzie snoring softly beside her, when the message box appeared.

Stony: Herman?

Herman: I'm here.

Stony: I found some stuff, but I don't think you're going to like it.

Herman: Gee, that's comforting. How bad is it?

Stony: Bad enough to make me wish I'd never taken this job, I can tell you that. My boss isn't just playing off the prophecy angle; he's actually orchestrating things to make all those prophecies seem to come true. He's got a solution to the world hunger crisis, a way to bring peace to the Middle East, new medical breakthroughs that his puppet can take credit for, you name it. He's planning to rule the world within the next month, I swear.

Herman: Okay, but we knew he had to have some of those things, or he couldn't pull this off. What's got you so upset?

Stony: He's got everything set up. Herman, it's all in place and ready to go. There isn't any Number Two that I can find, but he's got people in place to make sure each aspect of his plan comes off without a hitch. He's got assets in place in every country including our own, and anyone who isn't willing to play ball his way is going to be eliminated. Care to guess who's first on that list? I'll give you a hint: he lives in the Vatican.

Herman: Wait a minute, he's going to assassinate the pope? I thought he was after some European leaders? The Pope isn't in the file you gave me the other day.

Stony: No kidding. Think I would have left that out if I'd known about it? I just found this stuff, and it's scaring me to death.

Herman: Got any timeline? Anything we can use to try to head it off?

Stony: Not yet, working on it. Thing is, I've been reading his internal messages, and he's got people in the office who are working with him to pull this off. This plan of his is designed so that each individual part of it takes its cue from the one before, as in, item B can't happen until item A hits the news. If the pope is item A, like I think he is, then as soon as he's whacked, item B will be triggered, then item C, etc. As far as I can tell, he's got each item primed and paid for and ready.

Herman: Paid for?

Stony: Yeah. He's funneled billions of dollars from a dozen different countries into this project. Some of those countries have agreed to cooperate with his plan, because he's promising them special favors when it all goes down and he's BMOC!

Herman: Well, come on, Stony, there's got to be something we can do! What can you give me? There's got to be something!

Stony: First thing that comes to mind is to tell your old man to back off. As far as I can tell, the only one who can stop this from happening is the boss himself, so if he gets killed, we're SOL! He's already given everyone their orders, they're just waiting for their cues.

Herman: Then let's nail those people! I'm sure Sam could get someone to go after them, round them up so they can't do their jobs!

Stony: Thought of that, but there's a catch: I don't know who any of them are. The email addresses he's using are ones he set up. They're accessed through an anonymizer system, and scrambled so that you have to have an encryption key to read them. All these people need to do is log in the way he tells them to, and they can talk all day long without anyone ever knowing who he's talking to. Even his is a wild card. We couldn't prove he sent or received any of these emails.

Herman: Great. Thinking. You said you're reading his internal messages. Can you send messages out as him?

Stony: I thought of that, too, but so did he. Each of his operatives has a code word that he gave them in a face-to-face meeting. If he sends them any order to change plans, it has to contain that code word, and I have no way of knowing what they are. I figure he must have a list somewhere, but I can't find it.

Herman: I'm calling Sam. He needs to know all this, now. Don't go away.

Stony: I'll be here.

She slipped off the bed and took both the computer

and her phone out into the hallway. The cabin wasn't huge, but the loft it had once had had been expanded into a second floor, and she and Kenzie were sharing the first bedroom at the top of the stairs. Her mom had the other one up there, and Grace got the main one down on the ground floor. Poor George had to sleep on the sofa, but he said it was really comfortable.

She sank down onto the floor and called Sam, who answered instantly.

"Babe, it's me," she said, "and you gotta listen. You can't kill Chandler!"

"Yeah, we'd already figured that out," Sam said. "What made you think of it?"

"I'm talking to Gary, and he said Chandler's got this all set up so it's like a domino effect. Each part of his plan will go off as soon as the one before it does, and he thinks the first one is going to be the assassination of the pope. That's all set up, but he doesn't know when it's supposed to happen."

"Sheesh," Sam said. "Doesn't this guy ever quit? So, has Gary got any ideas how we can stop him, then?"

"Well, maybe," Indie said. "He says Chandler's got a list of code words somewhere, and all the people he's been sending orders to know that if he changes the plan, he has to give them their code word, the one he told them when they were together. If he doesn't use that word, then they'll know it isn't really from him, and the plan goes ahead. Gary can't find that list; if you can, then he could send out messages that would tell them all to stand down. It's not much, but it's what we've got."

Sam sighed. "Great. Well, you called at the right moment. We're just about to do our best to kidnap Chandler, so at least now we know what we need to try to get out of him."

Indie could hear the tiredness in his voice. "I wish I had something better to give you. I miss you, Sam. I want you to come home."

"I will, babe, I will," he said. "Just as soon as this is all over, I'll be home. Kiss Kenzie for me, and tell our mothers hello. And if your mom happens to get any advice for me from Beauregard, let me know, okay?"

Indie couldn't resist a chuckle at that. "I will, babe, I promise."

She hung up, and pulled the computer back into her lap.

Herman: Okay, I told him. He's going to try to get that list of code words out of Chandler.

Stony: Okay. Wish him lots of luck, because we all need it.

* * * * *

Sam scowled as he put the phone back into his pocket. "Indie's been talking to handler's computer whiz again. He says the plan is rigged so it will go off with or without Chandler, and the only way to stop it is with some code words that only Chandler knows. If we can take him and make him talk, we might be able to stop it

61

all. If not, then..."

"You're always so optimistic," Ken said, but Sam didn't even crack a smile. They had just watched as Chandler and an entourage of five men and a woman had left the restaurant and climbed into a small van to drive away, and Natasha was trying to follow and keep them in sight, while not getting close enough for them to be sure they were being followed.

"That's what we're dealing with," he said. "Chandler's got agents in place all over the world I guess, and each one knows that when something particular happens – one of the events he's set up – then that's their cue to make their event happen. The only way to stop them is a message from Chandler that contains a code word he gave them, and I guess it's a different word for everyone. If we can get that list, then Gary can send out the messages that will stop it all. Otherwise, nothing can stop it before it's too late."

Ken and Natasha looked at one another, and Ken shook his head. "Geez, this thing gets better and better. I thought I was just out to stop a guy who was trying to bring on globalism and destroy our national sovereignty, and now we're dealing with the fact that we're after a madman who makes Hitler look like a Boy Scout." He sighed, and turned in the seat to look at Sam. "What you're saying is that if we'd killed him back in DC, or even last night, we'd still have to deal with whatever it is he's got set up, right?"

"Something like that," Sam said. "I don't know if whoever he's got set up as a puppet is still gonna take charge if that happens, or if it's just that all his disasters will go off and we'll be dealing with the aftermath, it could be either way. All I know is that if we want to stop these things, we need that list of code words or whatever."

Natasha shrugged her shoulders and looked angry. "That settles it, then. We have to take him alive, and we have to make him talk. No other way, right?"

Sam shook his head. "Nope," he said. "No other way."

They continued to follow the van, which went out of Jerusalem on Highway 60, traveling to the north. They'd been on the road for about twenty minutes at that point, and the van seemed to be cruising along at a steady clip. The road was empty out that far, and Sam found himself just watching the scenery flow past.

"Hey, hey, what's this?" Natasha asked. "They're pulling off, turning onto a dirt road. Do I follow?"

Sam sat forward, and grunted. "If you do, they'll know we're here and following. We'd have to move right in, and to be honest, if we try to take them on our own, I'm not sure we'll be able to do it. There are seven of them and three of us, and that doesn't strike me as great odds."

Ken nodded. "I agree with Sam. Go on by, go another half mile and then turn around. We'll have to park and walk in, most likely, just to do a recon. Try to see what we're dealing with here."

Natasha nodded and moved into the left lane, slowing to let the van get further down the road and away from the highway. By the time they passed the road it had turned off on, the vehicle was almost out of sight. Natasha pressed the accelerator, then, and sped up to get to where she could safely turn around.

It was almost three minutes before she got to a place where she could do so, and then she hurried back to the entrance to the road. There was no sign of any vehicles, so she turned in and followed the track for a short distance, then pulled over and stopped behind a small hill, out of sight of the actual road itself. Sam had his phone out and was looking at the area on Google Earth.

"Okay, we've got a good-sized residential area off that little side road up ahead, to the north. If they've gone into there, we'll never find them. If they went straight ahead, on the other hand, there's nothing much but a whole lot more desert. I see a couple of big buildings out there, no clue what they might be."

"Hang on," Natasha said, "and I'll see if I can find out." She took out her own phone and dialed a number. "Itzak, it's Tasha. Get my GPS location and tell me what's around here that might interest DGSE agents. Of course I'll hold, idiot, what else am I going to do?" She covered the mouthpiece and leaned over to look at Ken. "Do you know how hard it is to get good people lately?

No, of course you don't, you work alone. Never mind, but trust me, it's—yes, I'm still here. Yes? Really? Well, well, isn't that just interesting? Thank you, Itzak, I'll make it up to you later." She hung up the phone and smiled. "Well, one of those big buildings is the research lab of a joint French-Israeli company named Fire Flower that's been working on a process for making a better fuel grade methanol than what's currently available. Some of the unofficial reports that Itzak has seen indicate that they've been successful. If he's right, then they can now produce a pure methanol fuel that any car can run on, and for less than a nickel a gallon. The process is simple enough to be set up just about anywhere there's a surplus of vegetable matter to use for fermentation."

Sam had both eyebrows about as high as they would go. "That's great news, unless you own stock in Exxon, but how does it help us?"

Ken chuckled. "Sam, you must be getting tired," he said. "Chandler wants to be the force behind the Antichrist, so he's got to be able to solve all the big problems facing the world. Fuel and energy are two of the biggest ones there are. Safe bet that it figures in to his plans." He turned to Natasha. "Do you know how far up the road it is?"

"Not me," she said, "Sam's the one with the maps. Sam?"

Sam looked at his phone. "There are two buildings, and I don't know which one it would be. One is about a mile and a half ahead, and the other is, oh, twice that. Three miles, give or take a thousand feet, I'd say. And that one is surrounded on the photo by crop fields, so that's probably the one we want." He looked out through the windshield as if he could see the building in the distance, even though there were hills blocking the view. "I wish I'd grabbed that carbine. We might have had a chance for some sniper work."

Natasha grinned. "If we do, there's something in the trunk that's even better. M21, the old American sniper rifle. I snagged it yesterday, just on the off chance we might need it. It happens to be one of Kenneth's favorites."

"Sure is," Ken said. "One of the finest long range weapons ever made, in my humble opinion, and I mean bar none! Get me to somewhere I can see down onto that building, and I can pick 'em off as fast as they can come running out!"

Sam looked at him for a moment, and then smiled grimly. "You're giving me ideas. Let's go get a better sense of the range, shall we?"

Natasha put the car back into gear, and they moved toward the building where they hoped to find Chandler.

4

The building was right where Sam had said it would be, and they found a place to hide the car from view that was less than half a mile from it. Ken and Sam climbed a hill and found a spot for Ken to hunker down with the rifle, and then Sam went back to the car and Natasha.

"Here's what I've got in mind," he said. "I've got an idea on a way to spook Chandler out of there and herd him toward Ken. Once they're away from any possible help, Ken's gonna pick off his escorts, starting with the driver to stop them. Once they're isolated, then, you and I will move in and take him alive."

She nodded as if this were what she'd been expecting to hear. "Kenneth is good," she said. "He'll take out the others, and all we should have to deal with is Chandler, himself. We should go on past the building, just in case they try to go out that way. Even with handguns, we should be able to send them back toward Kenneth."

"Then let's do it," Sam said. Natasha started the car and put it into gear, and Sam stayed low in the seat as they passed the building where Chandler was apparently playing God. Sam looked at it, then glanced at Natasha. "Natasha," he said, "I've got an idea."

They went half a mile past the structure, and found another small hill to park behind. Sam took out his phone and scrolled through the recent call list until he found the one he wanted, then told the phone to dial it.

A tired and nervous voice said, "Hello?"

"Hi, there," Sam said. "This is James Davis, remember me?"

Sam heard a swallow on the other end of the line. "Whole lot better than I want to," Gary Stone said. "Can't say I was expecting you to call me tonight. Is there a reason I shouldn't hang up now?"

"Just the fact that you're in too deep to quit now, and eventually you're gonna need me and my friends. Listen, kid, I need one little favor and then I'll do my best to leave you alone, got it?"

A sigh. "What's the favor?"

"I need your boss's cell number, the special one he uses just for his secret contacts. I want to give him a ring."

"Whoa, whoa, whoa, no way! If I were to give you that, he'd know it was me. See, it isn't one number for everyone, it's one phone with a dozen or more numbers that ring to it. As soon as it rings, he knows who's calling.

If I give it to you, he'd know you got it from me, and I wouldn't live ten minutes after that."

Sam rubbed his eyes, thinking. "Okay, then help me out, here. He's in a building, and I know where. I want him to come out of there in a panic, so that my people and I can pick off his henchmen and take him into custody to get you a certain list of code words. How can I make that happen?"

It was Gary's turn to think, and Sam could hear the wheels turning in his head as he mumbled to himself. "Let me ask you, didn't you have a man from HS with you, who got killed when you went after him?"

Sam scrunched his eyes. "Harry? Harry's not dead, as far as I know. He was wounded, but pulled through." He glanced at Natasha, who was nodding.

"Okay, good, even better. Yesterday, he called me and wanted me to find out all I could about you and your friends, and he thought Harry Winslow was dead. He asked me to find out if there were any official sanctions against him, which there aren't because everyone is too afraid of him. I'll call him right now and say that I just got a message that Winslow isn't dead, and has sent a team out after him. Tell me where he is, so I can make it sound like he's only got a few minutes to get out, and he'll run right to you. But, let me tell you, man, if you miss this time, I'm done! Don't call me again, and I mean it!"

Sam grinned. "Deal. He's at the Fire Flower labs in

Israel. Tell him Harry's alive, and that there's a military strike team coming to take him into custody. Say he's got fifteen minutes to try to get out of sight again. We'll do the rest."

He heard the kid sigh once again. "Man, you'd better, cause I want to live long enough to get old! I'll make the call as soon as I get off, so be ready." The line went dead a second later.

Sam called Ken and told him to be ready, then cleared his phone and watched the building. He was standing on top of the car, using the zoom function of his phone's camera like binoculars, so that he could actually see the entrance doors.

He counted less than a hundred seconds before those doors burst open and several people came flying out. He'd expected to see Chandler and his six escorts, but more than a dozen people were scrambling into cars, and it was only by chance that he actually spotted Chandler getting into a sedan, rather than the van that had brought him there. The van was the first vehicle out of the parking lot, followed by that sedan. Sam punched his phone to get Ken back on the line, praying that he'd answer.

"Yeah, what?" Ken growled.

"Chandler, he's not in the van! He's in the red sedan behind it, just him and one other person, the driver!"

"Got it!"

Sam cut the call and hopped down onto the hood

and then the ground, swinging himself into the open door. "They went toward Ken, let's go!" Natasha slammed the car into drive and floored the accelerator, spraying dirt and sand and rocks behind them as she roared out of where they'd been hiding.

Up the road, Ken had been busy. As Sam and Natasha came into view, they saw the van lying on its side off the edge of the road, and the sedan was nosed into a hump in the sand. Chandler was out of the car, lying on the ground. Natasha slid to a stop close to him, and Sam was out of the car with his Glock aimed at Chandler's forehead.

"Freeze, you crazy bastard," he said, and Chandler looked up at him with a face full of confusion. It cleared up a second later, and Chandler laughed.

"Good lord," he said between guffaws, "you actually turned my own people against me? I never would have believed that little geek could have the balls, but that's the only possible explanation. He spooked me right into your plans, didn't he? That little snot! Wait till I get my hands on him!"

Sam shook his head, as Ken came jogging slowly toward them. "You're not going to get your hands on anyone, Chandler," he said. "You're going with us, and you're going to tell us something we want to know. After that, if you've been cooperative, then we'll see what we can do about getting you a comfortable cell in a super max prison somewhere. If not, then you'll simply die very painfully. That choice is entirely up to you."

He bent down and frisked Chandler, taking his cell phone and a small revolver, then grabbed his shirt and hauled him to his feet, wincing as his bad hip complained about it. The man was still chuckling.

"Prichard," he said, "you're such a dreamer. How many times have you guys tried to take me out, now? And can you even guess how many others have tried? Shamash has always protected me from you and your kind, and he always will."

Sam shrugged. "Sorta looks to me like he's taken a hike on this one, Chandler. In case you hadn't noticed, you're a prisoner, now, not the guy calling the shots."

Chandler shook his head, his smile undaunted. "I don't know why, but Shamash wants me with you for the moment, or you'd never have gotten me. But I can guarantee you this, Prichard – there's something coming that will take me back out of your hands. Shamash isn't going to allow his work to be stopped, not this close to seeing them all come to fruition."

Sam shoved Chandler into the back seat, and then climbed in beside him as Ken got into the front. With both of the men aiming handguns at him, Chandler was docile, but he kept smiling.

"So," Sam asked Natasha, "where to?"

The woman laughed softly. "Oh, trust me," she answered, "I know just the place." She drove back toward the highway they'd left earlier, and turned back toward the city of Jerusalem when she got there. They'd been back on it for about three minutes when they saw a number of Israel Police vehicles racing back the way they'd come.

Sam looked at them as they passed, then turned to Chandler. "If those were the guys you were counting on, I think you're out of luck."

Chandler looked amused. "Shamash is a god, Prichard, the most powerful of them all. He doesn't need puny mortals to do his will, but sometimes he chooses one he finds worthy as a special warrior, or a messenger. I'm one of those, and that's why he's protected me all these years. When he sends someone after me, it won't be local cops, trust me. It'll be one of the lesser gods who serve him, and you'd better hope you don't piss him off at the time. Gods don't like to be annoyed."

Sam stared at Chandler and shook his head. "Jesus, you're really crazy, aren't you," he said, and Chandler began to laugh again.

Ken looked at Sam. "Can't I just kill him?" he asked, but Sam shook his head.

"Not just yet," he said. "We need those code words; it's the only way to stop his plans."

Chandler's laughter became raucous. "Code words? And you think you can get them out of me? You stupid idiots, why would I give them to you? All I'd have to do is give you some fake words, and then all of my people will know that you've got me, and then they'll ignore even me if I tell them to stand down, which I wouldn't do. You're screwed, gentlemen, and if you had any sense at all, you'd know it. All of the works I've set up for Shamash will come to pass, just as he told me they would, and there is nothing you or anyone else can do to stop them, now!"

Ken looked at Sam. "Just lemme kill him, please? He's right, we can't ever be sure we got the right codes, so there's pretty much no chance we're gonna get anywhere with this plan. If I kill him, then at least we know he won't live to enjoy any of it."

Sam looked at Chandler. "The worst part of that is, you're right," he said to Ken. "We've got him, but it won't help us in the long run, because he can actually use us against ourselves." He studied Chandler's face for a moment, then leaned back against the door of the car. "Go ahead, kill him," he said, and Ken grinned as he pressed the barrel of the rifle against Chandler's forehead.

Chandler's eyes went wide as he saw Ken's own widen in delight, and realized that he was about to die. He stared as Ken's finger began to squeeze, and then closed his eyes.

The rifle went "click," as the hammer fell onto a firing pin that had no cartridge to strike, and suddenly it was Ken who was laughing loudly. He turned to Sam. "Oh, man, you shoulda seen your face! You didn't think

I was really gonna pull the trigger, did you? You thought I was bluffing!"

Chandler was gasping for breath, but he began to smile again. "You see?" he said. "Shamash protected me! You were out of bullets, and you didn't know it! Shamash protected me."

Ken stopped laughing and looked at Chandler, then held up his right hand. In it were three bullets. "I didn't run out, you jackass, I unloaded. I just wanted you to realize that I could kill you any time I want, and your little fake god isn't gonna stop me when the time really comes. Give me half a reason, and that time will come right soon. Now, you wanna rethink your opposition to giving us those code words? Seems to me you'd rather sit in a cell and be alive than let me put a bullet through that empty head of yours."

Chandler forced his smile to stay and firm up, but there was something about it that said he was shaken. "I'm not giving you anything," he said. "You can't stop me, and you can't win. In fact, I'll give you one last chance to join me, how's that?"

Sam was watching him closely, and didn't buy his act of bravado. "You're such a fake, Chandler. I don't think you even believe your line of crap about Sham-ass, or whatever you call him, you just want a name to hang on the stuff you're doing."

Chandler sneered, as Natasha made a hard left turn and then accelerated again. "Well, then, you need to check your source of information, Mr. Prichard. Shamash has quite a following, in reality, although it's kept somewhat secret. We followers are known as Babbarites, and we worship him in a number of powerful rituals. His magic is far greater than any other in the world, and we..."

"Aw, shut up or I'll tell Ken to kill you for real," Sam said, and Chandler closed his mouth with a shrug. Sam turned to Natasha. "How much farther to wherever we're going?"

"About five more minutes," she answered. "It's a small warehouse that's been set up for things like this, when we've got to keep someone isolated and might need to dispose of them permanently. It's swept for any kind of surveillance every few days, and I made sure it was clean again this morning. I've got keys, and no one will come near it for at least a couple of days. That's how long we've got to crack him."

Chandler laughed again, and Sam scowled. "I don't think we've got that much time," he said, staring into the madman's eyes.

They arrived a few minutes later, just as she had said they would, and she used a key to turn a switch that opened an overhead door, then drove inside. A button inside on the wall let her close it down once again, and then the lights came on.

"Bring him and follow me," she said, and Sam dragged Chandler out of the car. Ken got out on his own, moving stiffly after the workout of hurrying down to the car earlier. They all followed her into the back rooms that they could see.

Natasha went to a cabinet at the back wall, and reached inside to press a button that was disguised as a screw head. As soon as she closed it again, the whole thing began to rise up from the floor, and an empty box appeared before them. "Get in," she said, and led the way. Sam grinned as he realized that it was some kind of an elevator, one that he was sure must take them into a cellar below the main floor, but when it descended, he saw that the cabinet above was several inches wider in both directions, so it stopped in its original position as the elevator continued on down. It had a small light on its ceiling, and they could see each other clearly.

The shaft was smooth, but it was obviously cut from natural rock, and Sam guessed that it must have descended at least twenty feet or more. When it stopped, Natasha stepped off and into what appeared to be a fair-sized room. She apparently knew where the light switches were, for they were suddenly in bright light that overwhelmed the little one on the elevator cage. That one winked out a moment later.

There was a table in front of them, and several chairs. Some of them were austere, but some appeared to be quite comfortable, and Ken dropped into one of those. He had left the rifle in the car, but had his pistol in his hand. "So, now can I kill him?"

Natasha grabbed Chandler and shoved him toward one of the plainer chairs, and Sam saw that it had straps on it. Together, he and Natasha strapped Chandler down at wrists and ankles, and then Natasha went to a small cabinet that stood beside the table, reaching in to withdraw a box that was full of different kinds of cutting implements. She set it on the table and turned to Chandler.

"Mr. Chandler," she said, "we haven't been formally introduced. I'm Natasha Minsky, and I work for the United States government. My role there is sort of flexible, but let's just say that one of the reasons they hired me is because I have a certain expertise in extracting information from reluctant sources. Since you have worked for the CIA, I'm certain you're not going to be one who believes that line about how we never resort to torture, so I'll give you the courtesy of explaining what's about to happen." She showed him the contents of the box, then pointed down to the floor beneath the chair. "As you can see, there are drains under your seat. That's because you're going to be losing a lot of blood, Mr. Chandler, and it has to go somewhere. I'm going to skin you, you see, a tiny bit at a time, until the pain reaches the point that you can't withhold the information we want. I'd tell you that you could save yourself a lot of suffering by simply giving us that information now, but it wouldn't be true. I'd skin you anyway, just to make sure you had been telling the truth."

Sam stared at her, unsure of what to think, and then

she turned and took a pair of rubber gloves from a box full of them that he hadn't even noticed on the table. He guessed that she must have taken it from the cabinet, as well, and when she had them on, she selected a thin knife and turned to Chandler.

"I'm not bothering with antiseptic, Mr. Chandler, because you're not going to survive, anyway, at least not for long." She stepped toward him, and Chandler's eyes got wider and wider until she held the knife just over his right forearm.

"Remember, Prichard," he said, his voice high and shrieking, "if you let her do this, you're throwing away any chance to be on the winning side! If you help me now, and stop this madness, I can find a place for you that will be high in my councils! You can be a powerful man, Prichard!"

Sam looked at him, and then noticed that Natasha was looking his way, and appeared to be amused. Inside, he was horrified at what she was about to do, but something in her manner told him that she wasn't bluffing. He swallowed his bile, smiled at Chandler and said, "Go for it, Natasha."

The screams that permeated the building were louder than Sam had ever imagined possible, but Ken just sat there. Sam sat down in another armchair near him, and a few moments later, he saw that Ken had fallen asleep. Chandler's screams, as Natasha removed one square inch of skin at a time, cutting a square in the flesh of his chest with the blade, and then using a pair of pliers to grab it and rip it away, grew more intense with each piece she took but Kenneth Long merely slept through it all.

Sam couldn't sleep. He waited until Natasha had stepped back after removing about the fourteenth piece of skin, and caught her attention.

"You're not asking him any questions," he said, and she shrugged.

"At this point, he still thinks something is going to happen to save him, so he'll make stuff up to try to appease me. He has to reach the point of knowing that there's no hope, before he'll be willing to talk, and then he won't be asking me to stop and let him go—he'll be begging me to kill him and make the pain end."

"And that's when you'll know he's telling the truth?"

"Oh, he'll probably never tell the truth. Sam, he's got nothing to lose, now, except his whole plan. If he tells you what you want to know, then he's beaten, and you've won. Until he believes he's going to die, he won't tell you what you want to know because he hopes to get out of here and wants to see your face when you realize he beat you. Once he accepts the inevitability of his own death, though, then all he wants is to have that one final victory, that final revenge, to die knowing that you failed to stop his plans. He's not going to tell you the truth, Sam."

Sam stared at her. "Then—then why are you doing this to him?"

"Because he deserves it," she said simply. "If you can't handle it, then leave. The keys are in the car, and I can have someone come for me when I'm finished." She glanced at Ken, still snoring in the chair. "Take him with you, would you? He's a bundle of bad memories, for me."

Sam stood there for another long moment, and then turned and kicked Ken's chair. "I'm leaving. Are you coming, or staying here?"

"He's going with you," Natasha said. "I told you that."

Ken looked at Natasha, and then at Sam. "I guess I'm going with you. Where are we headed?"

"To find Harry," Sam said, as he stepped into the elevator cage. "And pray like mad that he knows what to do next."

"Shaare Zedek Medical Center," Natasha said as the elevator began to rise. "Room three twenty."

Sam nodded, then looked once more at Chandler. The madman was glaring at Natasha, but he began to whimper as she turned to him with the knife raised again. He began to scream as the elevator ascended into its shaft, and Sam was thankful when the sound died out a moment later.

"She says he's never going to tell us the code words," he said to Ken, and the assassin nodded.

"Most likely he won't," he said. "That's all he's got left to use against us. Oh, he might, when the pain gets bad enough, but there's no way to know for sure. If we try to use whatever he gives us, it's odds on that we'll be shooting ourselves in the foot."

"So we're beaten? Is that what you're saying?" They stepped out of the elevator and walked toward the main room, where the car was waiting, as the elevator and cabinet descended into place once more.

"We're not beaten until it's too late to stop things," Ken said. "As long as something hasn't happened yet, then there's always the chance you can stop it. That's what we've got to look at now. Do we have any leads on who any of his people are?"

They got into the car, with Ken taking the wheel. "Not that I know of," Sam said. "All I know is that this Gary kid thinks the first thing that's supposed to happen is that the pope gets killed, and that's the thing that signals everyone else to set off whatever they're supposed to do – the other assassinations, the cruise ships, the school attacks, all of it."

Ken pushed the button that opened the overhead door to the street, and then started the car and put it into gear. "Let's go see Harry," he said. "Maybe he'll have some kind of an idea what to do, because I'm fresh out."

5

They drove into Shaare Zedek Medical Center forty-five minutes later, following GPS directions on Sam's phone. The parking lot was big, and by the time Ken found a parking place, another twenty minutes had passed. They got out of the car and made their way inside, both of them limping for different reasons. Ken even looked a bit like he belonged there, with some of his bandage showing through the collar of his shirt.

A stop at the information desk told them where Harry's room was located, and they rode a more civilized elevator up to the third floor. Signs that were printed in several languages made it easy to find the old man, and Sam had to laugh when he heard Harry's voice even before they got to his room.

"I can assure you, my dear, this is not the first time I've ever been in a hospital," came the old Southern drawl, and Sam grinned. "Just hand me the damned thing, I know how to pee in it!"

Sam and Ken turned the corner into the room, and saw a very frustrated young nurse standing there in front of Harry. "But, Mr. Winslow," she was saying, and only turned around when she saw the big smile spread across Harry's face.

"Sam, boy!" Harry said, "And I see you've still got that other rapscallion with you, so at least I know you survived! No one here would tell me a blessed thing, and I've been going nuts all day! I was just about to call Indie, and see if she knew anything, but I was scared to death it would be bad news! Come on in, maybe you can convince this little girl that I don't need her to hold my wee wee for me while I make a whiz!"

Sam chuckled again, and turned to the nurse. "Honey, if he says he can do it, I'd just let him. Arguing with him always ends up with something bad happening, and you just seem too nice for that."

The girl started to say something, but them gave Sam a look of disgust and shoved a urinal into his hands. "Fine, he's all yours," she said in deeply accented English. She turned and stomped out of the room, and Sam tossed the urinal onto the bed.

"Harry, it's good to see you're alive. The last time I saw you, your eyes were glazed over and you looked pretty dead, to be honest. When Natasha said you were alive, I didn't quite believe it."

"Now, Sam, I've told you before, I'm a hard son of a

gun to kill. Believe me when I say it's been tried by the best, but I'm still here. The question is, did we get anything done? What's the situation on our problem?"

Sam and Ken both looked to be sure there was no one in earshot, while both of them sat in chairs that were close to the bed. Ken said, "We missed him at the cafe, Harry, but then Sam's wife found him for us at the home of a Libyan diplomat. Natasha's surveillance people tailed him this morning to a restaurant down by the French Embassy, and we were able to tail him after that to a place out in the desert. We were about to try again when Sam's wife called; seems that computer kid of Chandler's had found some pretty heavy stuff, that his entire plan is set up like dominoes. One part goes off, that triggers the next, and so on. As far as we know right now, the first phase is the assassination of the pope, but we don't know when or how or who; we've got nothing but a message to Chandler saying that it's on, but no way to ID the sender. According to Gary the Wonder Kid, the only way to call it off is to get a list of code words Chandler gave to his ops, words that can confirm that a message really is from him, so we snatched Chandler instead of killing him. Tasha's working on him now, her specialty."

Harry sat there with a long face. "He won't give up anything," he said. "Once she gets hold of him, all he'll be able to think of is finding a way to beat us, and that means never giving us a way to stop his plans." He sighed, and leaned back against the raised bed. "Sam," he said, "all we know is that the pope is at risk, right?"

"Right."

Harry cleared his throat. "I can only think of one plan that might have any merit to it, but I'm not sure how you're going to feel about it."

Sam looked at the old man, and then rolled his eyes. "Since when have you ever cared what I thought? Give it to me, Harry."

The old man grinned at him. "That's the spirit, boy. I've been saying for weeks now that if I ever had a son, he'd have been you! Okay, here it is. Take Ken and head for Rome, and call that beautiful wife of yours and have her meet you there. Get that kid of Chandler's, too — you'll probably need them both. My idea is this: I know one person at the Vatican I trust, and I can get him to listen to you, but the best he might be able to do is give you some possible suspects for whoever Chandler is working with there. Between the four of you, you might be able to figure it out and track him down in time to stop the assassination—assuming it's not too late already."

Sam sat there for a moment, and then shook his head. "Harry, you're asking me to put Indie in danger, again. I can't do that. I almost lost her over Darrel Unger, Harry. I can't risk actually putting her into a case like this one."

"But, Sam," Harry said, "that's why I told you to take Ken with you. His job is to keep her and the other kid safe, while you track down Chandler's agent. Now what

I'm hoping is that his man there might have information on some of the others, and that he won't be as fanatical as Chandler. If he's got intel you can get out of him, then we stand a chance of putting an end to this whole situation before anyone else can get badly hurt. Can you see my logic, Sam?"

Sam sat there and stared at him for a long time, and none of them spoke. Ken let his eyes wander around the room, but he didn't look directly at Sam, and Harry merely stared right back at Sam. Several minutes passed, and at one point the nurse came back in, but Harry lifted the empty urinal and waggled it at her, so she left again without a word.

Sam finally sighed, and took out his phone. It was almost noon, so it would be just about six a.m. back home. Indie had called him early that morning, and then again a couple of hours ago, so he knew she'd been awake most of the night. He looked at Harry.

"You arranging the flights?" he asked, and Harry grinned and nodded. Sam dialed his phone and waited a moment for Indie to answer.

She got it on the second ring. "Sam? Babe, are you okay?"

"I'm fine, honey," he said. "Listen, I was wondering—how would you feel about a trip to Rome?"

There was dead silence on the line for almost five whole seconds, which is a long time on an international phone call. "Sam, did my mother call you?" Indie asked him, and he squinted in confusion.

"Your mother? No why—oh, don't tell me! Beauregard?"

"Huh! Mom came in here a few minutes ago and said Beauregard had just told her you might be taking me on a long trip, way across the ocean. I thought maybe she meant a vacation or something, but..."

Sam sighed. "Babe, I can't tell you all of it right now, but I need your help in Rome. Ken and I are going to be leaving here shortly and heading there, and we'll be bringing your pal Gary in, too. Harry's hoping that between the four of us, we might be able to stop the disasters Chandler had planned."

Indie smiled into the phone. "How do I get there?" she asked simply.

"Harry will make arrangements," Sam said, "and he'll send word to George, I imagine. I guess you'd better start packing, baby. Kiss Kenzie for me, and tell her I love her and we'll be home soon. Love you!"

"I will," Indie promised, "and I love you more!" She hung up before he could engage her in the ritual argument over who loved who more.

"One down," Sam said. He dialed again with the phone on speaker, and smiled when the phone was answered with a groan.

"Please, please, please don't tell me you blew it!" Gary said, and Sam wondered if he was hearing tears in the kid's voice.

"We got him," he said, and the sound of a sob came through loud and clear. "Thing is, he isn't going to give us what we want, so we've got to find another way to stop his plans from happening. We need your help, buddy."

There was a silence for a moment. "Help how?" Gary asked.

"I'm with my old pal Harry, and we'd like to bring you into our team. We need you to fly to Rome and help me and my wife try to track down the one who's supposed to arrange the pope's assassination. Are you willing to do that?"

Gary was quiet for a moment. "Can your old friend Harry do anything to make sure I don't get burned along with the rest of Chandler's people, if we pull this off?"

Sam raised his eyebrows at Harry as he said, "I'm pretty certain that if you help us out, we can guarantee you immunity from any kind of prosecution." Harry nodded, but stopped when Gary went on.

"Prosecution?" he squeaked at Sam. "Who the hell is worried about prosecution? I want to know if you can keep me alive!"

"Yes," Sam said. "You come on with me, and I'll put you under protection. Deal?"

Gary hesitated for a moment, then, "Well, I guess so. Do I use my real passport, or make one up?"

Harry waved for Sam to bring the phone closer. "Young man, my name is Harry Winslow, and I've been advised about what a help you've been. I'll arrange for someone to come and get you within twenty minutes. He'll identify himself by saying that he has an extra pizza. Go with that man, and he'll get you to Rome safely."

"An extra pizza? God, you spooks are so corny, couldn't you think up something better than that? How about saying, 'your presence is needed in the land of the Caesars,' or something like that?"

"Gary, just go with the pizza guy, and I'll see you in Rome. I'll fill you in then." Sam hung up, ending the call before he could get frustrated. He looked at Harry.

"So, the plan is for me to get Indie and the whiz kid to Rome, and try to use their skills to ferret out who Chandler's man in Rome might be, then get him to tell me who else he knows of who was involved, right? You do realize that this is a pretty flimsy plan, don't you, Harry?"

Harry smiled. "I don't think so, Sam," he said. "If there's one thing I know about you, it's that you're a cracker-jack investigator, and if the clues are there, you'll figure out who the bad guy is in time to stop him. Go to Rome, and set those two to digging. If they turn up any clues at all, then I know you'll find the bastard, and then you can either make him talk, or track him back to fine others. Either way, I think it's our best hope to stop the things Chandler has set into motion."

"Thing that bothers me," Ken said, "is why he'd have it all set up to go ahead if he wasn't there to enjoy it. I'm not saying he should have expected to be caught or anything, he's a maniac, and they never believe anyone can beat them—but most of them don't put something like this on a timetable, they want to give the order themselves. That's what's odd about this mess, to me. Why wasn't he planning to give the order that started it all, so he could watch it all unfold on the news from somewhere comfortable?"

"Maybe he was," Sam said. "Maybe the guy in Rome, if Gary's right and the assassination of the pope is the first shot, maybe he's waiting for Chandler's call to go ahead."

Ken shook his head. "He said there was no way to stop it, even if we did manage to kill him, remember? That means he knew it would go off even without him. No, for some reason, he didn't worry about being in a place where he could be safe and comfy while he watched his plans destroy the world as we know it. It was set up so that it would begin whenever some special condition was met, and if we could figure out what that condition is, then we'd be ahead of the game."

Sam looked from Ken to Harry and back. "Maybe the Pope is going to give a speech, or put himself in position to be accessible, and that's what makes the assassination possible."

"That might be it," Harry said. "The Pope is often giving speeches and making appearances. Your job would be to figure out which one it might be, then, and how the assassin might plan to do it. If you can get a lead like that, then it could be a game changer." He hooked a finger at Sam. "Give me your phone." he said. "I need to book you a flight, and then you boys need to go and get packed."

Sam handed over the phone, and listened with half an ear while Harry told someone to take the two of them to Rome on the soonest possible flight, even if it meant making a special one. Then, he began issuing orders about getting Indie and Gary onto flights, and Sam grunted when he heard Harry rattle off Gary's address without even slowing down.

Apparently he had the clout to back up his demands, because the person on the other end agreed to everything Harry wanted. Harry hung up and looked at Sam.

"You've got two hours. Go to your hotel and get your things, then get to the airport. You'll meet a man named Jackson at the diplomatic flight line, and he'll take you past everything. Don't take weapons, of course, they and everything else you might need in that line will be provided when you get there." He leaned back and closed his eyes. "Did they tell you I got shot in the chest? Doctors said the bullet went clean through my lung, and they thought I was dead when I arrived. But my heart was still going strong, so they took me on into surgery. For the record, this is the eighth time I've been shot, and the third time I've almost been declared dead on the scene." He opened one eye and focused it on Sam's face. "The next time I volunteer to join you on a mission, Sam, do me a huge favor and tell me to butt out, would you? I'm too old for this crap!"

Harry was snoring a few minutes later, when the nurse came back in. She took the still-empty urinal from his hand, rolled her eyes, and stormed back out of the room.

Sam and Ken left the room right behind her, and took Natasha's car back to the hotel. They got their bags, checked out and drove back to the airport, leaving all of the firearms in the car's trunk, and then found the diplomatic line once again. A skinny fellow was standing there, holding a sign that said, "Sam."

"You must be Jackson?" Sam asked, and the guy smiled as he looked up from the magazine he was reading.

"I am," he said. "You must be Sam and Ken, right? Just follow me, please, I've already got you cleared and your plane is waiting." He turned and went toward a door that led out of the terminal, and the two men followed him.

Their plane turned out to be an Air Force cargo plane, a C-5 Galaxy, and Ken groaned.

"What's the matter with you?" Sam asked.

"Cargo flight," Ken said. "We're probably gonna be sitting on boxes or mailbags. This will be one of the worst flights of your life."

"Oh, I doubt that," said Jackson. "There's no cargo. From what I was told, whatever you're doing has presidential authorization to utilize any resources, so this flight was ordered up for the express purpose of carrying you two to..." He looked at a card in his hand. "To Rome. You'll be sitting in the passenger cabin, on the upper deck, along with the flight crew. The seats aren't bad, I've ridden in them myself."

A loadmaster crewman met them at the entrance to the aircraft and showed them to the passenger cabin. They took seats that would leave them off by themselves, and the crewman told them they'd be airborne within fifteen minutes. They heard the big engines coming to life a moment later, and Sam said, "It's like any other flight."

There was no answer so he looked over at Ken and found him sound asleep already. Sam grinned and leaned his own seat back. They were on their way to Rome, with no idea what might be waiting there. Sam whispered a prayer for strength and guidance, and a special one asking God to keep Indie safe through this mission.

His phone rang, and he looked at it to see Natasha's number. He answered quickly.

"Hello?"

"I just thought you'd want to know," Natasha said, "that Chandler died ten minutes ago."

Sam swallowed. "Really?" he asked. "Did you get anything out of him?"

"Well, he never did give me any code words, but I

got one thing I thought might be useful. It was his last words, actually, as he was realizing that his phony god wasn't going to save him after all. He said, 'She'll make all of you pay for this.' I tried to ask him who he meant, but that was all I got."

"She? Sounds like there's a woman involved, then. Could he have been planning to put a woman in charge?"

"Considering that he was going up against a large number of Muslim nations, I'd find that unlikely, but I suppose it's possible. I mean, theoretically, whoever he was putting out there was supposed to unite the nations and bring peace right?"

Sam thought for a moment. "Natasha," he said, "what happens to him now?"

"I've already run what was left through a grinder, Sam. He's in the sewers, on his way to a fitting destiny for a pile of crap like him."

Sam hung up and put his phone back into his pocket. He leaned back and tried to get the mental image of Chandler, with half his skin removed, out of his mind. It took a while.

The flight from Tel Aviv to Rome took just under four hours, mostly because the military flight was forced to route around certain areas in the countries which it overflew. There were certain areas where the airspace was restricted to nonmilitary aircraft, so any flights with any type of military designation had to go around them.

They landed at da Vinci airport, in Fulmicino, Italy, and found a young woman waiting for them when they got off the plane. "Mr. Prichard? Mr. Long?"

They admitted to being the men she was looking for, and let her lead them through the airport. They had to flash their phony diplomatic passports at one point, but were waved on through as if the person who looked at them just wanted them out of his hair.

"My name is Maria," the girl said in an obvious Italian accent. "I have a car waiting for you, according to my instructions. We have arrangements made at a hotel, and I will drive you there, but after that you'll need to drive yourselves around. I was not told to provide you with the driver, so once I deliver you to your hotel, someone will come to pick me up." They followed her through the terminal and out toward the parking areas, where she led them to a somewhat rough looking little sedan. "I was told to inform you that everything you might need is in the luggage compartment. I am only a civilian employee, so I don't have clearance to discuss your reasons for being here. I was told that if you need any further assistance beyond what I can give you, that I must contact one of my superiors."

They climbed into the car, with Sam in the back seat and Ken riding shotgun. "It's been a while since I've been in Rome," Ken said. "What hotel have you stashed us in?"

Maria started the car and drove them smoothly out

of the parking area, toward the street. "You've been put into the Royal Palace Hotel. It is a surprisingly luxurious hotel, one that your country has a contract with for visiting diplomats and dignitaries. I've never stayed there myself, but I've been told that it's a wonderful experience."

"Separate rooms, I hope," Sam said. "My wife will be joining me later, maybe tomorrow or tomorrow night."

"Actually," Maria said, "you are in a suite with adjoining rooms. I was told that there are others coming, a woman and another man, and to make sure that there were sufficient rooms for all of you. Unfortunately, the largest suite they had available has only two bedrooms. The two additional men will have to share a room."

"That's okay," Ken said. "If he snores, I'll just shoot him."

Maria made a face, but said nothing. Sam laughed. "Ignore him, he's all talk."

"You didn't say that in Israel," Ken said.

"In Israel, we weren't being driven around by a young lady with no security clearance. Hush up, now. You can talk all you want after we get to our hotel rooms. I'll just shut the door, so I can ignore you."

They made their way through the streets, with Maria handling the car like an expert. Ken grinned at her. "You drive pretty good," he said. "How long before we get to the hotel?"

"Well, the hotel, of course, is in Rome," she said. "That's about forty-five minutes away, and by the time we get through the city itself to the hotel, you're probably looking at about an hour. Are you hungry? I was told that if you wanted to stop to eat before you go to the hotel, I was to take you wherever you want to go."

"Tell you what," Ken said. "Why don't you pick us a spot to eat? Choose someplace you'd like to eat, since this is all going on the government credit card anyway."

Maria glanced at him, shyly, but with a grin. "I know a place, a place I've always wanted to go to eat but could never afford. Would that be all right?"

Ken reached into his pocket and pulled out his stack of credit cards, looking them over. "Yeah, I think that'll be fine. It's not some kind of fancy place that only serves weird stuff, is it? I mean, do they serve steaks there?"

Maria nodded enthusiastically. "Oh, yes sir," she said. "They have the finest steaks you have ever tasted. I have heard many who visit your Embassy speak of it, but I've never been able to go there. Are you sure this won't get you into trouble?"

Sam laughed. "Honey," he said, "trouble is the last thing we're worried about right now. If we can make your day by taking you out to dinner at this place, then maybe it'll chalk up something good on our karma. Worth a try, anyway."

She smiled brightly. "All right! This is exciting!" She drove on, talking rapidly about the restaurant and all that she had heard of it. By the time they got to Rome, Sam felt that he and Ken could probably make a living by simply telling people about this fabulous restaurant, and then charging them a few dollars to give them the name and address of the place. They'd heard all the wonderful features so many times that he was sure it would be impossible for them to forget any of it.

The place was called Primo al Pegneto, and Sam was glad they were using Ken's funny credit cards. Each course of the meal cost more than an entire meal at any place he'd ever been back home in Denver. The food was divine, however, and he happily ate his share of it.

* * * * *

Indie was packed and ready, and Kenzie was already figuring her take for putting up with it, this time. When both her parents were gone, it meant she had to stay with her two grandmothers, Grandma Grace and Grandma Kim, and staying with them meant getting lots of shopping in. Grace had a fair amount of money, and loved spending it on Kenzie, which meant that Kim had to spend some of her own money to keep up, and Kenzie had it made when they started competing!

"Tell Daddy I miss him, and I want him to come home with you," she said to Indie. "I don't like it when he has to go away to work. Don't we have enough bad guys here for him to catch?"

Indie smiled, and let her eyes go wide. "Yes, we do, but sometimes there are people who are so bad that it takes someone special to catch them, and that's when they call your Daddy in. This bad guy was so bad that Daddy had to chase him halfway around the world, and now he has to go to another place to catch him, and he needs Mommy to help. Isn't that exciting?"

Kenzie nodded, her own excitement level still building on thoughts of a trip to the mall. Since George was taking Mommy to the airport, Mr. Harry had said it was okay for them to all go home, so Kenzie and her Grandmas would be going to Grace's house. Kim lived there in Grace's spare room, anyway, so it wouldn't be a huge issue.

Indie kissed her daughter goodbye, hugged her mother and mother-in-law, then got into the limo's big back seat. George hurried around to the driver's seat, and they were off, bouncing along the gravel road until they got down to the main paved road that led back toward the Interstate.

Rome! Among the many places Indie had always dreamed of one day visiting, Rome held a special spot in her heart, for it was one of the most well-known places in all of history. The Caesars, the Coliseum, the Vatican— there were so many incredible places to visit and see, and she found herself hoping that she'd get the chance to do some sightseeing while she was there. Maybe, if they were able to finish up whatever Sam had to do somewhat quickly, there would be a couple of days they could spend just being tourists. Indie would love that!

The ride to the airport, with one stop at Sam and Indie's house to pick up her passport, took a couple of hours, and then George handed her off to a young woman who led her through the diplomatic processing line, and fifteen minutes later she was on a plane. The airplane wasn't as big as the one she and Sam had flown on to Hawaii, but it was still pretty large, and she was surprised when the flight attendant had her sit in the front row, then began closing the doors.

"Excuse me?" Indie asked. "Aren't there other people on this flight?"

"No, Ma'am," the attendant replied, shaking her head. "This is a specially authorized flight, and you're the only passenger. That's all I was told. Can I get you anything before we take off?"

Indie shook her head, her eyes wide. A whole airplane, just for her? What on earth was going on?

The flight took off, and the attendant asked again if Indie wanted anything. "Maybe something to drink, for right now," she said. "Are we flying straight through to Rome?"

"Oh, no," the attendant said. "This flight is only going to Philadelphia, then you're getting on another plane there that'll take you to Rome. Again, that's all I know."

Indie swallowed and smiled. She took the half size can of Coke and tiny glass of ice she was offered, and sat back to enjoy the flight.

The flight was only a little over three hours long, so Indie landed in Philadelphia at just after three in the afternoon, eastern time. She let the flight attendant lead her to the diplomatic gate, where another young woman was waiting to take her into another room.

"Hi, you're Mrs. Prichard, right? I'm Stephanie, with HS. I work with Harry, sometimes, when he needs something from the home office. He told me to meet you here and make sure you get introduced to your fellow passenger." She led Indie through a second doorway, and a short, skinny kid stood hastily to his feet. Indie broke into a big smile.

"Stony?" she asked, and Gary Stone's eyes went wide.

"Oh, wow, are you Herman?" He smiled, and Indie dropped her bags and wrapped him in a hug. "Wow, you're even prettier than I..." He trailed off, and his face turned red.

Indie giggled. "Gary, I'm Indie," she said, "and I'm delighted to finally meet you! When they told me we'd be working together, I was tickled! I've never gotten to work with another real hacker before. This is gonna be exciting!

Gary got out of the hug, and stood there trying not to let his shyness get the better of him. It wasn't easy, especially when one of the most beautiful girls he'd ever seen was standing there smiling at him, but he kept his cool until Stephanie announced that it was time to get them onto their plane.

This time, they were going on a commercial flight with British Airways, but because of their diplomatic status, they were boarded first. They were seated together, and even though Gary had the window, he willingly gave it up to Indie when she said she wished she'd gotten it. They chit-chatted a few minutes about normal things—Gary talked about his boring life, and Indie showed him pictures of Sam and Kenzie on her phone—as the other passengers were boarded, and then the announcement of impending takeoff came over the loudspeaker. The engines began to whine louder, and the big plane moved backwards for a moment, then began rolling toward the runway.

Indie was always amazed that something so huge could move so fast, but when the scenery alongside the runway began moving past at racetrack speeds, she felt her face split into a big smile. A moment later, the nose of the plane rose into the air, and then the rumbling of the wheels fell silent as she found herself on her way to the land of the Caesars and the Gladiators. Gary was leaning forward to look past her, and she grinned at him.

"We're on the way to Rome, Gary," she said, and he smiled back.

Too bad she's already married, he thought.

6

Rome is a city full of history and atmosphere, one that is so blessed with art and beauty that it has become a cliché as far as tourism is concerned. A visit to Rome is merely to be expected when one is going on vacation to Europe, for no one should ever pass up the opportunity to see all the wonders that exist there.

Sam Prichard was as amazed as anyone else by the sights of the ancient city, and he and Ken had spent most of their first afternoon and evening acting like automotive tourists, just driving around in their beat up sedan. He didn't want to get out and wander around too much, considering that they were both armed and there seemed to be police just about everywhere.

They'd taken the two suitcases from the trunk up to their suite, and Sam had been tickled to find another Glock in one of them. He had threaded its holster onto his belt within a second, and then spent ten minutes filling four magazines and stuffing them into pockets.

Sam had his Homeland Security ID, which theoretically authorized him to carry a concealed weapon in any country that was an ally of the United States, but he didn't want to test it. Ken, on the other hand, had several different forms of ID, none of which were real, that would almost certainly get them both locked up if they were scrutinized too closely. Sam didn't want to test those, either.

There's only so much a man might want to do, however, without his wife, at least in a place like Rome. They cruised around the city for a few hours and then went back to their hotel. Sam didn't know how long it would be before Indie arrived, but he wanted to be refreshed and sharp when she got there. He hadn't seen her in days, and he'd missed her terribly.

For what was reported to be a luxury hotel, the Royal Palace had some amenities there were normally found only in discount lodgings. One of those was a laundromat for the guests, and after one whiff of the inside of his travel bag, he just picked it up and carried it to the laundry room. The whole thing, duffel and all, got dumped into the washer, and he fed it coins until it was ready to start. Another machine dispensed laundry detergent, and Sam was sure he paid it far more than the actual prices listed, just trying to get the box out of the stupid machine.

A half-hour later, he transferred it all into the dryer,

which resulted in another battle with the coin slot. Since the dryer started up, Sam figured he must have won. Another hour saw him as the true victor, as he carried a bag full of clothes back up the elevator and didn't worry about whether the other passengers might be offended by the odor.

Clean clothing in hand, Sam went for the shower, blissfully unaware that Ken was pulling the pillow over his head in the other bedroom as Sam sang his heart out about how beautiful his wife was. The shower, unfortunately, wasn't sufficient as instrumental music to back up his vocals. Ken told himself that he would have a talk with Sam about this issue come morning, just like he'd done every time he heard Sam singing in the shower.

The sound of the water and the singing ended abruptly, and Sam vigorously toweled himself dry. He slid into his clean underwear and a T-shirt, then made his way back to his bedroom, fell onto the bed, and rapidly slipped into dreamland. His dreams, however, were of the screams Grayson Chandler had uttered as Natasha carved bits of skin from his body. Sam would never forget either the sight or the sounds that he had experienced that day, and only the knowledge of the things Chandler had planned to do to thousands of people, including many thousands of children, allowed him to go back to sleep after the nightmare woke him up.

In the next room, Ken wasn't having any trouble

sleeping. While Sam was new to a world where you sometimes ignored the Geneva Convention in order to save lives, Ken was right at home. This was his element, and he was very good at moving through this world. Men like Chandler, who thought they could literally rule the world, were ultimately terrified of men like Kenneth Long, who would let nothing stop them from doing what they believed was the right thing to do. You could not dissuade them, you could not escape them; the only thing you can do with men like Ken was to kill them, but that wasn't often an easy thing to do.

Both of them slept until the sun came through their windows in the morning, and then each of them rose, looked out the window, then rolled over and went back to sleep.

* * * * *

Their flight landed at da Vinci airport at just after nine thirty in the morning, and Indie and Gary were hustled off the plane before anyone else. This time, it was a young man who met them as they were brought into the terminal.

"Hello, and welcome to Italy," he said. Unlike Maria, he had no discernible accent, which made sense just a moment later. "My name is Joshua Smith, and I've been assigned to get you to your hotel. I understand you'll be meeting the rest of your team there?"

Indie extended her hand, and Joshua took it. "Hi,

Joshua," she said. "I'm Indiana Prichard and this is Gary Stone. Yes, we're meeting my husband and another man here this morning."

Joshua smiled as he nodded his head. "Then, let's get you on the way! From what I understand, whatever you're up to is pretty important. Let's not keep the others waiting. If you'll follow me, we'll go collect your luggage, and I've got a car waiting right out front."

"Sounds great," Indie said, and Gary only nodded as he followed along. Joshua led them through the airport terminal to baggage claim, past the diplomatic line where they only had to flash their passports at a clerk who was just as bored as the one who waved Sam and Ken through the day before, and out to a waiting limousine. The two of them climbed into the back, while Joshua stowed their luggage in the car's big trunk. A moment later, he climbed in with them and tapped on the glass that divided the car into two segments. The driver apparently got the message, because the car moved out smoothly. Moments later, it was on the road toward Rome and the Royal Palace Hotel.

"Your team is being housed at the Royal Palace Hotel in Rome," Joshua said. "I'll warn you that, although it is considered a fairly luxurious hotel, this isn't going to be the most awesome hotel experience of your lives. The plumbing rattles, the air conditioning is sporadic at best, and rumor has it that at least a half-dozen ghosts are wandering through the hallways. On the other hand, thanks to a special contract with the

United States government, it has the best Wi-Fi you'll ever find anywhere in Europe. That's because it has its own dedicated satellite uplink connection, and that's tied right into the hotel's Wi-Fi. Now, most guests don't get access to that particular Wi-Fi connection, of course, but Mr. Winslow made it clear that he wanted you guys to have the fastest and most powerful Internet connection possible. Well, in Rome, that means the Royal Palace Hotel."

Indie laughed. "Gee, all that and a haunted hotel, too? What more could a girl ask for?"

"You can ask for whatever you want," Gary put in, "but when Uncle Sam is paying the tab, what you're going to get may be completely unrelated to what you asked for. I learned that months ago, when I first took this job. I had to throw a royal fit just to get a decent computer to work with. Anything that has to go to the government accounting office for approval is likely to get chopped and slashed as if it was an actor in a low-budget ninja movie."

Joshua chuckled, and he and Gary did a fist bump. "Amen, brother, you got that right! I had to raise Cain this morning just to get this car. Your other guys were picked up in one of our old beaters. Don't get me wrong, the car will run fine, but it looks like crap. Somebody said they would need a car to get around in, so that's what they got assigned to them. Personally, I think that stinks."

"Yeah, well," Indie said, "if I know my husband, as long as it has four wheels and a motor, he'll be happy with it. He loves cars, any kind of cars."

The conversation dawdled along, but Indie and Gary were more interested in the view outside the windows of the vehicle. Coming in on highway A91, they were treated to some amazing views, including the Coliseum and the Trevi fountain, two of the most recognizable landmarks in the world. It wouldn't have surprised Indie to know that her husband had driven past both of them several times the night before.

They arrived at the hotel at ten thirty on the dot. Indie had insisted that they not call ahead, because she wanted to surprise Sam. Sure, she admitted, he knew she was coming, but he didn't know exactly when she would arrive. She warned Gary and Joshua both to just shut up and let her enjoy herself.

Fortunately, Sam and Ken had finally given in to the sun's insistent demands that they get up, and were seated under one of the umbrellas in front of the bistro next door to the hotel. When the limo pulled up in front of the hotel's entrance door, which was merely a single door cut into a solid wall, both men took notice. When Gary stepped out of the car, they recognized him, got up and hurried over just in time for Sam to catch Indie in a hug as she got out.

"Oh, my goodness," Indie said. "Oh, Sam, I was trying to surprise you!"

"Baby, just seeing you is surprise enough! I was blown away when Harry told me to call and ask you to meet me here, but this is big enough and important enough that I can understand why he'd want you on it with me." He kissed her, then turned to Gary. "So, kid, I gather you're on our team, now?"

Gary shrugged, but nodded his head. "Looks that way," he said. "Listen, I've brought along everything I could snag out of Mr. Chandler's computers, notes, everything. But I've been pounding on this stuff for a couple of days, and I just haven't come up with any answers. I'm not sure why they wanted me over here with you, but I'll do whatever you tell me to do."

Ken patted his shoulder. "That's all we can ask of you, youngster. Hey, we're just grabbing breakfast, you guys hungry?"

Joshua had climbed out with them, and unloaded their luggage. That done, he was standing by without interrupting. He took this cue to speak up. "Okay, it looks like I've done my job and delivered you where you're supposed to be," he said. "I gave you both my card, if you need anything you can reach me on the phone number there." He turned to Sam and Ken and extended a hand. "Gentlemen, it's rather obvious that I can leave these good folks in your hands. If you need anything, they know how to reach me. Whatever you're up to, I wish you all the best of luck, and I mean that very sincerely." He turned and closed the back door of the limo, then stepped up and climbed into the front seat with the driver. A moment later, the car pulled away.

"Well, the guy could at least have given me the chance to thank him for bringing you to me," Sam said, "but Ken's question still stands. You guys want some breakfast?"

"I'm starving," Gary said. "I'll tell you a secret about those overnight flights—they figure since it's overnight, they don't need to feed you a real meal. They give you a snack, instead. I need more than a snack, I'm a growing boy!"

Sam grinned. Indie nodded, and said, "I'm not a growing boy, but I'm definitely hungry. Should we take this stuff to your room first?"

They all agreed that it would be a good idea to carry all of their luggage up to the suite, so the four of them made a procession of it. Indie had brought two suitcases, some of which contained extra clothing for Sam, as well as her carry-on with her laptop in it. Gary, on the other hand had only one suitcase full of clothes, but he had two more cases full of electronic gear that he said he brought along, "just in case."

Indie was delighted to find that she and Sam would have a room of their own, and managed to make Gary turn red by warning Sam that she planned on making him make up for lost time later when they went to bed. Poor Gary, on the other hand, decided he would rather sleep on the couch in the sitting room than share a bed with a professional killer. Ken didn't help by joking around about needing someone to cuddle, and he finally apologized to Gary after Sam told him he was being a jerk.

"We can put everything away later," Indie said, "let's get downstairs to the food! I hope it's good!"

"No kidding," Gary said. "On the other hand, it won't take much to be better than the cheese sticks and pretzels they gave us on the plane. The pretzels were bad enough, but I think the cheese was at least twenty-five years old."

As they got into the elevator, Ken quipped, "Hey, don't you know that cheese gets better with age?"

"Then maybe it wasn't cheese. I mean, to be honest, I couldn't really tell for sure. It was sort of yellow, but it was more gooey than cheese should be. At least, I thought so."

"Hey, I didn't eat any. I left that stuff alone," Indie said.

The bistro wasn't much as far as bistros go, but they did offer a light breakfast menu that included eggs and sausage. The sausage was Italian, and spicier than what most Americans are accustomed to, but all four of them thought it was delicious.

"So, okay," Indie said, "all we've got, then, is a general clue that the pope is going to be assassinated, right? So how do we figure out when and where?

Anybody got anything on that?"

Sam shrugged. "Not quite yet," he said, "but Harry gave me a number to someone he knows at the Vatican. He told me not to call until you were here, and that you and Gary would figure out why. Got any inkling on that?"

"That's an easy one," Gary said. "That means he wants a tap on the guys phone line, so that we'll know if he calls anyone after you make contact. I'd say it's pretty good odds that he'll be calling somebody as soon as he's off the phone with you."

Sam looked at him. "But why? If he's a friend of Harry's, why would he be calling someone else?"

Gary looked at each of them in turn, and then shook his head. "I thought you guys knew who you were up against," he said. "Since you brought me in, I'm guessing that my old boss is no longer among the living, but that doesn't change the fact that he was a genius at this kind of crap. Remember that he spent years and years studying how terrorists work, and looking at the mistakes they made. He's not going to leave any loopholes in his own plans, they're going to be so airtight that you can't pierce them with a missile, let alone anything else. We're dealing with a man who could look at Hitler's entire operation, see the flaws in it and easily write an operational plan that would've made it a smashing success. If Osama bin Laden had had half of Grayson Chandler's brains, we'd all be Muslims by now. Just because he's dead doesn't mean he's beaten, trust me on this. Anyone he had working with him is not going to stop being scared of Chandler just because he's dead."

"You're talking about his dead man's stash, right?" Ken asked.

"I'm talking about a whole lot more than that," Gary said. "Chandler had people all over the freaking world who did nothing but make sure that other people did what Chandler wanted them to do. These folks aren't on a payroll, they don't collect a paycheck every Friday, they get paid in power. Chandler gave them enough knowledge to make sure they could always accomplish whatever he wanted them to do, and then he made sure he had enough evidence of what they did to see to it they were buried if they ever turned on him. He has that system so well-built that just being dead won't stop it."

"But do we have any idea who these people are?" Ken asked. "You can tell us all day long that he has these people, but unless we know who they are that does us no good. What else have we got on them?"

Gary shook his head. "I could identify a few of them, but not many. The point, though, is that these aren't the people that we're looking for right now. The people I'm talking about are the ones that those people are looking over their shoulder for. I can assure you, just as sure as we're all sitting in Rome, that the people who are going to carry out these plans for Chandler have not one, but two separate and complete motivations. First, they want to make sure they are in the power elite when all this goes down, but second, and just as important to them, they want to be sure that they're not on the target list when it's over. Anybody who gets in the way, or who doesn't do what they're supposed to do, is going to be on that list." He pointed a finger at Sam. "You call that friend of Harry's, but not until we got everything set up so that we can see who he calls afterward. I'll guarantee you, he's going to be calling someone, and that will give us another lead. Considering we don't know how soon this is all going to go off, I'll take any lead we can get right now, won't you?"

Sam nodded. "Absolutely," he said. "I'm with you, a hundred percent. We've got to find some way to get to whoever's behind the assassination of the pope. If that's the trigger, then we need to know who the trigger man is, and right away."

Indie leaned forward. "Gary," she said, "what about the people in this guy's office? He may not make any phone calls at all—the people watching him could be right on top of him all the time. What about that situation?"

Gary looked at her, and shrugged. "You could be right," he said. "There's not a list of Chandler's muscle out there anywhere, at least not one that I'm aware of. All I can tell you is that we need to ID this guy, the one you're supposed to call, as quickly as we can. Then we can be all over him, watch every move he makes until he leads us to somebody who leads us to somebody, etc.,

etc. Geez, it almost sounds like you're on a witch hunt. That's how they use to track witches down, back in the dark ages, by getting one person after another to point fingers. As long as they could point at someone else and claim they saw that person doing something evil, they got to walk away. It was the poor woman who couldn't or wouldn't accuse someone else who ended up burning at the stake."

"If that's what it takes," Ken said, "then so be it. We don't have the luxury of time, this is all about to start happening. If we don't come up with some answers, and real soon, people are going to start dying. I'm not Catholic, and I'm not all that crazy about the pope, but I don't want to see him get killed."

"Nor do I," Sam said, "but I'll be honest enough to admit that I'm a lot more worried about those thousands and thousands of school kids, not to mention the innocent people on the cruise ships. The Pope, the politicians, people who choose public life always know, somewhere in the back of their minds, that assassination is one of the risks they run. People on a cruise and kids in their classrooms should never have to worry about things like that."

"I agree with Sam," Indie said. "Yes, we need to stop the pope getting killed, but we have to remember that this is just a step on the way to stopping all the rest of the killings. If I understand all this correctly, it's the killings, and their aftermath, that Chandler was counting on to put his people in power, right? So, whoever it is that's expecting to step into that position is already in place, somewhere. He's just waiting for his cue in this big script, and then he can step up and say whatever it is he supposed to say to make people believe he's the new Messiah, right?"

Sam nodded. "Right. Although, there is something new that indicates that his new Messiah might be a woman, rather than a man." He looked sideways at Ken. "The last words Chandler said was that someone he called *she* would make us all pay. Sounds like maybe he has a woman groomed for that position."

Gary looked thoughtful for a moment, his eyes half closed as he ran this new data through his mind. "A woman?" He asked. "Holy cow, surely it couldn't be..." He shook his head vigorously, as if trying to clear a mental image he didn't want to see.

"Gary?" Sam asked. "Gary, what are you thinking?"

Gary looked him in the eye, and Sam pulled back a bit in surprise at the look of pure terror on the boy's face. "Look, I don't know anything for sure," he said, "so this is nothing but conjecture, but I can only think of one woman who would want the kind of power Chandler was offering, and who might be willing to allow these kinds of atrocities to happen in order to get it. If I were to say that I'm thinking of a certain ex-First Lady, I'd bet it wouldn't take you five seconds to figure out who I mean."

Sam, Indie and Ken all sat back suddenly, and their eyes all went wide. Indie was the first to speak.

"Oh, come on," she said. "I know there are lots of ugly stories about her, but get real. She'd have to be willing to sacrifice thousands of innocent children, and I just can't imagine any woman who could do that."

Gary shook his head. "Okay, something you need to get through your head is that we aren't dealing with men or women here, we're dealing with people who want power. They don't think like you and me, and a human life, to them, is nothing but a bargaining chip. You've heard the old conspiracy theory, how it was really her that ordered the fire that killed all those Branch Davidians in Waco? Well, according to documents in Chandler's files, that ain't just a theory, it's a fact."

Ken nodded his head. "I've heard from other sources that that was true," he said. "I'll even be honest enough to tell you that I know personally of several times when her name was invoked as the authority behind a kill order, both when she was first lady, and later as Secretary of State. And before you get all humane on me, let me tell you that I know of things just as bad that were done by lots of other politicians from our country. It's like Gary said, human lives are nothing but bargaining points to people like that. Chandler was pretty much running the black market on power, buying and selling it as he chose, and I can guarantee you that every purchase and every sale involved the loss of human lives. If she's the one, I can't say I'd be all that surprised."

"Well," Sam said, "some of the conspiracy theorists have been trying to claim that she was antichrist for years now, so it's quite possible Chandler would've felt like she was ideal for the job. Still, we don't know anything, not for sure. I think we need to stick to what we do know, which is that our immediate goal is to find out who's behind the assassination of the pope."

Their breakfasts were finished by this time, so the four of them got up and went up to their rooms. Gary immediately began unpacking some of his gear, and Indie was fascinated by a lot of the devices he pulled out of his bags. While he explained each item to her, the others merely watched in silence.

"This thing? That's a Wi-Fi snoop. What that does is it logs on to any Wi-Fi network, and then records all the activity of every device connected to the network. Makes it possible for someone like you or me to go in and basically replay everything that happened on that network for however long the snoop was in place. We can run searches, look for files of any type, check download logs and even see what may have been downloaded, see any videos that may been watched — pretty much lets us know what everyone on the network was up to."

"Like an activity monitor," Indie said, "the kind of thing that big corporations use to see what their employees are up to online?"

Gary laughed. "An activity monitor is to a Wi-Fi snoop about like what a caveman would be compared to one of us. Pretty primitive, and not nearly as effective. If

I can get that gadget within range of any Wi-Fi network where, for instance, we might have a suspect who is likely to be checking his email or some such, and pound my way through passwords until I get it online, then within a matter of minutes we'd be able to read all of that suspect's emails, messages, virtual chats, see which dating sites he was playing around on and even check out books on his Kindle library account. Heck, we can probably order pizza with his credit cards. I brought three of those, because sometimes it's easier to put one in place than it is to retrieve it."

"Gotcha," Indie said. "What about that?" She was pointing at a small plastic box that had several different digital readouts built into it.

"That's a gizmo that only existed in science fiction novels until a couple of years ago," Gary replied. "That's what's called a code picker, and it's very useful for opening these high security doors that only open when you've got the right digital key in your pocket, transmitting a signal. It's the same principle as the new cars that don't need a key to start. As long as you got the appropriate transponder in your pocket or on your person, somewhere, all you've got to do is push the button and the car starts up. Well, assuming you want to get through one of those doors or start one of those cars, but don't have the transponder you need, this little gadget solves your problem. In a matter of seconds, it can pick out the right code that should be transmitted in order to open the lock or start the car."

Sam grinned. "I got a new nickname for you," he said. "I'm just going to call you Q."

Gary grinned back. "Want to know something funny? Q was always my favorite character in all the old James Bond movies, because he always had all the cool gizmos and gadgets. I think if I had half a chance, I could come up with even better stuff than he did."

"I'll tell you what," Sam said. "You do me right in this mission, and I'll twist some arms to try to make sure you get that chance. Deal?"

Gary let his grin broaden into a smile. "Oh, yeah," he said, "you got yourself a deal, there!"

"Okay, if we can bring the spy movie fan convention to a close," Ken said, "maybe we can move on to more important things. Like figuring out who it is we got to track down here in Rome, everybody up for that?"

"Of course we are," Indie said. "We're just figuring out where to start, right at the moment. Gary, what do we need to do so Sam can make his phone calls?"

Gary was setting up his computer, which was a whole lot bigger than Indie's laptop. It was portable, in the sense that it seemed to be built into a fairly large and very sturdy suitcase, but there was something about it that said it was years ahead of what she had.

"What on earth is that?" She asked in awe.

Gary grinned at her, a smug grin that said he understood exactly what she was asking. "Eurocom Panther 5SE," he said. "Twelve core Intel Xeon processor, thirty-two gig of RAM and 6 TB of hard drive space. This thing is an entire IT command center, all by itself. Heck, it's got eight different operating systems installed. I can run Windows, Linux—you name it and I've got it."

Indie stared at the computer for a moment, then turned to Sam. "I want one," she said simply. Sam grinned, and looked at Gary.

"Okay, just curious, but what does one of those puppies cost?"

Gary shrugged. "This one was specially ordered, and ran about twelve grand. If you don't need all the different operating systems, you can probably get one for less than ten."

Sam whistled. "Put it on your Christmas list, baby, and I'll see what I can talk Santa into. Meanwhile, let's get both your computers up and doing their jobs. Gary, you never did answer her question."

"Well, first things first," he said. "What we'll need to do is lock onto the number you're going to call, got that handy?" Sam dug out a piece of paper and passed it over to him. "Okay, now what I'll do is go into the major telephone service here, and do a highly illegal tap on that line." He sat down at his computer and began tapping on its keys like a piano virtuoso playing a master composition. Indie stood at his shoulder, watching everything he did. Sam noticed that she nodded a lot, as if approving of his actions or techniques.

A moment later, Gary handed the slip of paper back to Sam. "Okay, I've locked on to that number. What I've done, is built a virtual clone of that phone into this computer, so that I can hear and record everything that goes through that number. That includes touch tones, so any number that gets dialed on the phone will be displayed right here on my monitor. Okay, Mr. Prichard, you can call whenever you're ready." He plugged in a set of headphones and slipped them over his ears.

"It's just Sam, Gary," Sam said. "Okay, I'm calling now." Sam dialed the number from the paper into his phone, and then listened as it rang. It was answered a moment later by a man's voice.

7

"Hello?" The voice seemed slightly hesitant.

"My name is Sam Prichard," Sam said, "and I was given this number by Harry Winslow. He told me to call whenever I got to Rome."

Again there was a slight hesitation. "Well, Mr. Prichard," said the voice, with a slight but discernible Italian accent, "any friend of Mr. Winslow is a friend of mine. How can I be of service to you?"

"Well, I'm here on business," Sam said. "There's a situation that I've been asked to try to prevent, a situation that could have grave consequences for the entire world. Do you have any idea what the situation is I'm referring to?"

"I'm afraid that I do not," said the voice. "And worse, I have forgotten my manners. My name is Vito, Vito Mangione. Now, can you be a little more specific about the situation?"

"Is your line secure?" Sam asked abruptly.

"It is," Vito said. "You may continue."

"Okay, good," Sam said. "I've been working with Harry on a case involving a rogue American agent. This man's been orchestrating a plot to bring about a global government, actually following a great deal of biblical prophecy regarding the end times. Now, he hasn't been going at it from a Christian perspective, but was following some weird Mesopotamian religions, but it comes out pretty much the same."

"Following biblical prophecy? Are you talking about the Book of the Revelation?"

"Yes, exactly," Sam said. "The man's name was Chandler, and he was basically setting himself up to be the puppetmaster behind the antichrist and the false prophet. Now, that's how we would see them from the Christian world, of course, but he had a different viewpoint on it that fit his own religious beliefs. All I know about that is that he didn't see the end of the story the same way that we do."

Vito was quiet for a moment. "Chandler? I don't believe I've heard that name. Is it someone I should know?"

"Not that I'm aware of," Sam said. "The issue right now is that his plans involve creating some terrible disasters, acts of terrorism on a scale like we've never seen before. He designed his plan with several steps, each one worse than the one before, and each is triggered by the one before it. From what we've been able to determine, the very first step, the very first tragic event, is the assassination of His Holiness, the pope."

There was a gasp on the line. "But this cannot be! Who would do this terrible thing?"

"That's the problem were dealing with," Sam said. "We've got to figure out either who is arranging it, or who the actual assassin is, and the big problem is that we don't know when this is supposed to take place. Do you know if the pope has any special appearances scheduled in the next few days? Anywhere that might make him vulnerable to an attack?"

"Actually, no," said Mangione. "His Holiness is taking some time for personal reflection, and is not leaving his chambers for a few days. If this thing you speak of is to happen soon, it would have to be, how do you say it, an inside job? It would have to be someone with access to the papal apartments. That would be nearly impossible; I cannot imagine anyone who could have such access and entertain such thoughts."

"Look, Vito," Sam said, "I'm part of a team from the United States that's been assigned to stop this from happening. Officially, no country is recognizing any of the things that I told you as fact. This man Chandler had so many people involved in his plots, and has amassed so much influence, and you can read between the lines on that, that even our leading politicians are scared to go against him. Now, he, himself, is out of the picture;

unfortunately, he designed this plot to continue even without him or his involvement. What that means is that whoever is supposed to do these things is probably going to go right ahead with their part of the plan. The disaster is that if that person manages to bring about this assassination, it's going to set off another round of assassinations throughout Europe, followed by the sinking of some tourist cruise ships with all lives probably lost, and after that there will be an attack on American schoolchildren that I can't even describe."

"And how many, Mr. Prichard, are in your team? Do you have the sufficient forces to do what must be done?"

Sam sighed. "There are four of us. Two of us are computer and intelligence experts, and the other two are investigators. We're what you've got, and we need your help. Can you give us any kind of leads that we can follow, anything to help us try to get a jump on the situation?"

Once again, there was silence on the line for a matter of several seconds. "Mr. Prichard," Mangione said. "If it were not for the debt that I owe to Mr. Winslow, and the fact that you have invoked his name, I'm quite certain that I would consider you a lunatic and hang up on you. However, if Harry Winslow sent you to me, then he had a reason." There was humming on the line, as Mangione was apparently thinking through what he wanted to say next. "At this point, I don't know what to say. I'll need to think about it. I have the caller ID, can

I reach you at this number?"

"Yes," Sam said. "Vito, please understand that we don't have anyone else to go to in Rome, at least not right now. If you come up with anything, anything at all, and I don't care if it sounds crazy to you, call me. Let my people take it and run with it, and if there's something to it than it will give us a chance to head off this disaster. If not, well, that we will have eliminated one possibility, right?"

More humming for a moment, and then, "Very well. I will call you after I have given this some thought. Goodbye for the moment, Mr. Prichard, but I will call you again soon."

"Thank you, Vito," Sam said. "I'll talk to you then."

Sam ended the call, and looked at Gary. The skinny kid nodded, and pointed at his monitor while unplugging his headphones.

A dial tone suddenly could be heard through the speakers on the computer, and then there were a series of tones, as Mangione dialed a number. Sam touched Gary on the shoulder, and whispered, "Can he hear us?"

Gary shook his head. "Nope," he said. "It's a one-way connection. We can hear him and everything that goes through his phone, but he can't hear us at all."

Sam nodded, just as someone answered the call Mangione had made.

"*Salve?*" the call was answered in Italian.

"*Ho appena avuto un interessante chiamata*

telefonica," Mangione said, also in Italian. "*Un agente Americano retiene che ci sara un tentativo di assassinare Sua Santita!*"

"Well, crap," Sam said, "it'd be nice if we knew what he was saying!"

"He said he got an interesting phone call from an American agent who thinks someone might try to assassinate the pope," Ken said. "Or something close to that, my Italian's a little rusty."

The person Mangione had called said, "English. Did he say who it might be?"

"No," he said. "There is a group of them, special investigators from America. He said there was an American rogue agent who is essentially trying to take over the world, and he has laid a plan that involves the assassination of His Holiness."

"And do you believe there is any truth to the story?"

"This agent was sent to me by Harry Winslow," Mangione said. "That is enough to tell me that Harry Winslow believes it, and *that* is enough to tell me it must be true. If there is one man who always has his facts in order, it is Harry Winslow."

"Who is this agent? And did he tell you who the rogue agent was?"

"The man who called me was named Sam Prichard," Mangione said. "He said the rogue agent's name was Chandler. That's all I know at the moment."

"*Chandler? Oh, mio caro Dio!* And do you know

anything about where Chandler might be?"

"Prichard said that Chandler was no longer in the picture. I assumed that to mean that he is no longer alive. He also said that the problem they are facing is that Chandler's plans will go on with him or without him. They don't know who is behind the assassination, and have asked me if I can give them any leads. Carlo, I don't know what to do. If I go to His Holiness, I will probably not be believed, and I would have to expose these Americans. If our governments are turning a blind eye to this situation, then I fear what would happen if I try to take that path."

"Yes, yes," said the man called Carlo. "I agree completely. Vito, my friend, it appears that you did not know Chandler, and in that you are very fortunate. Chandler is, or was, a power broker. He makes it possible for people to gain power, whether that power be political, financial or in some other medium. Now, the way that he always did this was by making certain that he always had information that other people did not wish to see come to light. By merely threatening to expose that information, he could direct the paths of entire nations, sometimes even groups of nations. There are so many things in our world today that were conceived in his diabolical mind that I doubt I could possibly identify them all. If he has conceived the plan that you speak of, a plan that calls for the assassination of our beloved Holy Father, then I am forced to believe that that assassination will take place. He will have devised a means for its accomplishment that will probably be beyond our ability to detect."

Mangione sounded like he was about to panic. "But Carlo," he said, "we have to do something! We can't simply sit back and allow it to happen. What can we do?"

"I agree, I agree," said Carlo. "Let me think. Give me some time to think this through, and I shall return your call. For now, keep this between us and God."

"Yes, I will. Please, Carlo, if you can think of anything we can do, let me know."

The call ended, and Gary's fingers flew furiously over his keys. "What I'm doing," he said, "is getting a lock on our friend Carlo, there. Odds-on, he's about to make a call of his own, and I want to know who he calls, don't you guys?"

"Absolutely," Ken said. Sam nodded his agreement.

Gary sat back, and sure enough, a new sequence of tones was heard through the computer. There was ringing, and then the call was answered. This time, the person called seemed to be speaking native English.

"John Spencer," he said, answering the phone. "How can I help you today?"

"John, it's Carlo. I think we may have a problem."

"Carlo? What kind of problem? It's gotta be serious for you to call me on this line. Fill me in, buddy."

"Do you remember Grayson Chandler? There are

some American agents in the city who are claiming that he has orchestrated a plot to assassinate the pope. Do you know anything about this?"

"Holy Mother! I know Chandler, but I never heard anything about this kind of thing. Who were the agents, who are they with?"

"All I've heard is that Harry Winslow sent them," Carlo said. "The only name I've heard is Sam Prichard. I think he must be the agent in charge. The last I knew, Winslow was in America's homeland security agency, but I don't think anyone ever believed that's all he was doing. I mean, he's Harry Winslow, anyone who wanted to retire him would probably have to do it with a bomb!"

"Prichard, that's not a name I know. And this guy said Chandler was behind this whole thing?"

"Yes, and as far as I know, Chandler must be dead. There was something about the Americans being worried because the plan will go off even without Chandler being alive to see it through. John, do you know anything, anything at all, about a plan to assassinate His Holiness?"

Spencer was quiet for a moment, but then he came back on the line. "I don't know of anything," he said, "but I did run across something a few days ago. There was a package that came in, and I thought at the time that it seemed odd-sized and heavy. We were told to just hold onto it until someone came to claim it, and we were told to release it to the person who gave us a certain code phrase. That code phrase struck me as odd, also, because it was something about white smoke from the chimney. Since the pope is alive and healthy, I thought that was a strange choice for a passphrase."

"Oh, my dear God!" said Carlo. "There would have to be a connection—that would be too great a coincidence to be believable. Do you have any idea what was in the package? Was it a weapon of some sort, do you think?"

"I have no clue what was in it," Spencer said. "Could it have been a weapon? Possibly. I can't say that it wasn't, but I can't say that it was. The package was long, probably more than three feet long, maybe eight inches tall and ten inches wide, and must have weighed almost twenty pounds. It could have been a weapon. I mean, a package that size could hold just about any kind of rifle, including a disassembled sniper rifle. Man, I wish I'd paid more attention."

"What about the man who picked it up?" Carlo asked. "Do you know anything about him? Were you there, did you see who picked up?"

"No, I'm afraid I wasn't there. It was picked up day before yesterday, while I was out to lunch. Let me see if I can get Jeffrey to tell me anything. I'm going to put you on hold for a few minutes, okay?" He didn't wait for a response, but put Carlo on hold immediately.

Sam leaned forward and looked at Gary. "We got any idea who that Spencer is?"

Gary tapped a few keys, and then smiled up at Sam. "John William Spencer, Political and Economics Officer at the US Embassy to the Holy See. This guy is right smack in our embassy to the Vatican! And this Jeffrey he's talking about is Jeffrey Montrose, who would be his superior."

Indie had taken a chair and pulled it up close to where Gary was working on his computer at the desk, and was staring at him with wide-eyed wonder. Sam put a hand on her shoulder, and she turned to face him. "It's sort of like," she said, "like – like if you got to meet Sam Spade, or any other hero you might've had growing up. Gary might be a kid, but he's probably one of the best I've ever seen at the type of thing he's doing right now. I plan to learn a lot over the next few days."

Sam grinned. "I've got a hunch that might go both ways. From what I gather, you've done an awful lot without having all his fancy equipment and supercomputers. There are probably things he could learn from you, too."

"No doubt about it," Gary said. "We talked on the plane about a lot of things, and to be honest, I'm absolutely amazed at all she's done without any special equipment, or some of the training I've had."

Suddenly, the hold music they'd been listening to ended, and Spencer came back on the line. "Carlo? Listen, man, Jeffrey won't give me anything on the guy who picked up the package. I'm not sure what's going on here, but it's making me nervous. Can we meet up? Someplace outside?"

Carlos let out a sigh. "Let's go to the pizzeria," he said. "I can be there in about an hour. I just need to finish up a few things here, and then I can be on my way."

"Okay, Pizzeria Colombo?"

"Yes, that's the one. I'll see you there in an hour, maybe a little more." Carlo hung up the phone, but Spencer seemed to linger on the line for a moment longer. After a few seconds, the line went dead.

"Okay, kids, we're on to something," Sam said. "Do we have any idea who Carlo is?"

"Not a hundred percent certain," Gary said, "but I think it could be Carlo Santorini." He tapped a few keys on his computer, and a photograph appeared on the monitor. "According to a State Department security file on the Vatican, Santorini would be an assistant to the prefect of the papal household. Now, that sounds like he'd be way up in their organization, but that isn't necessarily the case. The prefect would have dozens, maybe even hundreds of assistants, all of them people who serve as butlers, and such, to the pope. There are also a lot of Benedictine nuns who work there, doing the cooking and cleaning and such."

"Then, if that's him," Ken said, "then he'd have access to the pope, himself. And you say there may be hundreds of people like him? Good God, all it would take would be one. If Chandler could turn one of these guys, all he'd have to do is slip something into the pope's food, or rig up a grenade to go off or something. How many freaking people are we going to have to check out, anyway?"

"As many as it takes," Sam said. "What I'm wondering is whether we should crash that little meeting of theirs at the pizzeria. Seemed to me that Spencer had something he wanted to say, just not over the phone."

Indie nodded her head in agreement with Sam. "Yeah, I sort of got that same feeling. It was like he knew something, but he was worried about who might overhear it, maybe even right there in his office. Might be worth somebody going out there and listening in."

Ken looked from her to Sam and back again, then nodded his head. "Okay. You two go. I look like crap, but you two could look like a couple of tourists. I think you should go and listen in, see what you can find out. I'll stay here with Einstein Junior, in case those guys make more weird phone calls."

Sam smiled. "Okay, sounds good," he said. "Indie, do you want to freshen up or change? It's a little early for lunch, and will still be early an hour from now. We can wander in and grab something to drink, act like we're just resting and cooling off. Taking a break, you know?"

Indie jumped up and got into one of her suitcases, kissed Sam on the cheek and hurried into the bathroom.

She came out a few minutes later looking like she just stepped out of the covers of a fashion magazine. She was wearing jeans and a designer T-shirt, and had done something quick and perfect with her makeup, brushed her hair (so that the clipped spot wasn't visible), and all three men froze and stared. Ken and Gary quickly regained their composure and looked away, but Sam just smiled as he looked at his wife.

"Baby," Sam said, "you get more beautiful every single day!" He looked around at Gary. "Can you give me the address of that pizzeria they mentioned?"

Gary gave it to him, and Sam posted into the GPS on his phone. They made sure they all had each other's phone numbers, and Sam led Indie down to where they had to stash the car in paid parking.

Having almost an hour to get to their destination meant that they had an easy forty minutes of free time, so Sam decided to show off a bit by cruising around the parts of the city he had become familiar with the night before. As he pointed out different landmarks, he couldn't help being delighted with Indie's reactions, and he found himself wishing that they really were just tourists. Being mixed up in this mess was frustrating enough when he was far from home and love, but now it was even more frustrating because he couldn't spend the time enjoying it with her the way he wanted to.

Still, cruising around the city with her was a lot more fun than it had been with Ken the night before. The

Italian drivers were just as crazy in real life as they always are in the movies, so they had their share of thrills and chills before they finally had to go on and find a place to park. Sam found a place not far from the pizzeria, another paid parking lot that took a few more of his coins, and then he and Indie strolled hand-in-hand up the street, weaving their way in and out of the crowds of natives and tourists who were always flocking around the streets this close to the Vatican. They found the pizzeria, slipped inside and took a table.

Carlo Santorini, decked out in the robes traditionally worn by members of the papal household, was already there, occupying one side of a booth. Sam and Indie pretended not to be watching him, and ordered soft drinks when the chance arose. It was as they were sipping them that a large man wearing an American-style business suit entered the establishment and sat down across from Carlo. The two men smiled at each other and shook hands.

"You seemed rather worried," Carlo said, "when we were on the phone. Did you learn something, John? Something you couldn't say at the time?"

Spencer spread his hands as if to say that he wasn't sure. "I honestly don't know," he said. "I was just told in no uncertain terms that the contents and recipients of packages that come through the embassy are none of my business. Now, that's the first time I've ever been told anything like that, and it was really quite a shock. I'm not sure what's going on, Carlo, and I would hate with everything in me to think that Jeffrey might be involved, but something just isn't right."

Carlo nodded, and Sam got the feeling that the man was worried. "Yes, yes, I understand," he said. "But, John, this warning is coming from your own countrymen. Chandler – oh, my, if Chandler has truly set his mind to something like this, and if he is willing to sacrifice the pope – John, I don't know what else to think but that the world has gone insane."

"No," Spencer said, "it's not the world that's gone crazy, it's just Chandler. On the other hand, is that really such a surprise? Power corrupts, and absolute power corrupts absolutely. Who was it that said that? Oh, never mind, it doesn't matter. The fact is that it's true, and Chandler has had the closest thing to absolute power that any man has known for decades, at least since Hitler's time. How could it not have driven him mad?"

"Agreed, agreed. What do we do now?"

"Well, it would help if we knew who these American agents are, how to reach them. I don't have any idea who might be running an operation against Chandler, because, frankly, I don't know anyone stateside who would have the nerve. You mentioned Harry Winslow, and I suppose he might be one of the very few who would have the courage, and probably isn't worried about anything Chandler might have on him. If all the old stories about Winslow are true, there just isn't much

I can imagine that would scare that old man." He looked around the room, and actually made eye contact for a split second with Sam before looking back at Carlo. "What do you think? Can you get us in contact with those agents?"

Carlo shrugged. "It was Vito Mangione who called me, and I don't know how much he actually knows. Perhaps he can reach them, all I can do is ask. What would you have me tell him? What should he say to the agents?"

Spencer sucked in his bottom lip for a moment, then smiled. "Tell him that if he can reach the agents, he should tell them that they have two allies inside the Vatican. I would suggest that you have him give them my name, and my personal cell number. You have that, right?"

Carlo nodded. "I have it," he said. "But do you think that is wise, to give it to them? If they know who you are, what if they were to contact your Jeffrey? If he is involved, that could be very bad for you."

"That's why I said my personal number," Spencer said. "Hopefully, they'll be smart enough to call me on that, and not try to come visit me at the office." He let his eyes roam around the room once more, and once again they met with Sam's.

Sam grinned, trying to look buffoonish, but there was a narrowing of Spencer's eyes that told him the man was not a fool. Sam winked at him, then rose, taking

Indie's hand and leading her over to where the two men sat. Sam slid in beside Carlo, while Indie smiled and sat beside Spencer.

"Mr. Spencer," Sam said. "I'm Sam Prichard, and this is my wife, Indiana. We are part of the team that you're discussing right now."

"Yeah," Spencer said with a grin, "I've been watching you while you were watching me, so I figured you must be. John Spencer, which you obviously already know. The fact that you're here tells me you had a tap on our phone, and I'm not even going to get into the legalities, or lack of them, on that. If what Carlo was told is true, we've got something a whole lot bigger to worry about than whether you had the right to listen in on my phone calls. What can you tell me, Mr. Prichard?"

"Well, I gather you know who Chandler was. What you may not have known was that he's apparently spent the last several years developing a plan to make it appear the biblical prophecy was all coming to fruition, complete with Antichrist, the false prophet, all of it. The gimmick was that he had it in his head that all of those prophecies really came from some old Babylonian religion, and that he could manipulate them to leave himself in the driver's seat. He has someone ready and waiting to fill those roles, while he would be sitting in the background pulling strings like a puppeteer. We don't know who that person is, and even though there is little speculation, we don't even have enough leads to even point fingers at anyone. What we do know is this. Chandler set up a plot in several stages, each of which is a bigger disaster for the world. It starts here, with the assassination of the pope. When that hits the news, the next item, which we believe is a series of assassinations around Europe, will be implemented. When that one is announced, it's the cue for the third, and again, we believe we know what that is. If we are correct, it will be the sinking of some cruise ships loaded with tourists and vacationers, most of them probably Americans. That one is particularly diabolical, because it's designed to make Americans turn on small Christian organizations the same way they now treat Muslim groups."

"But then it gets worse," Indie interrupted. "After that one, he has it all set up for what looks like a Muslim organization to attack a whole bunch of schools, while the kids are in class, using gasoline tanker trucks as suicide bombs. We're talking about the deaths of thousands of children, and the plot seems to be designed to make Americans scream for the complete annihilation of all Muslim people."

Spencer's eyes were wide, while Carlo's were closed and they could hear him fervently whispering in prayer. "Dear God," Spencer said, "you're talking about the opening salvo of World War III! An attack like that — there's nobody in the world who could prevent that turning into a global conflagration."

"Unfortunately, that's where you're wrong," Sam

said. "At least, that's what Chandler believed. Whoever his puppet is, he or she would step up and somehow bring peace to the world. Of course, that peace will come at the price of national sovereignty to every nation that subscribes to it. One global government, one ruler. Yeah, they'll dress it up in nice, pretty language about constitutions, and parliaments or Congress or what have you, but the real truth of the matter will be that Chandler's puppet, now that he isn't around to pull the strings, will be the de facto ruler of the whole world. That's what we're out to stop, and the first step is to find out who's behind the plot to assassinate the pope. We're hoping and praying that if we can do that, we can find out who's handling the next item, and so on until we find the actual puppets themselves."

Spencer stared at him, and then reached out a hand to Carlo. The old priest grasped Spencer's hand, as both men looked at Sam and Indie.

"I don't know exactly what we can do, and I can tell you that I have reason to believe that someone in the office I work in at the embassy to the Holy See could be involved in this," Spencer said. "But Carlo and I are old friends, going back to when I got my first job over here at the Vatican Embassy. If there's one thing I can tell you, it's that he can be trusted, and I'm pretty sure he would say the same about me. You've got two allies, right here. You tell us what we can do, and we're in."

8

"Okay," Sam said, "what we need to do is figure out who could have been on Chandler's payroll inside the papal apartments. That's assuming, of course, that the assassination attempt is actually planned for the next few days while the pope is not moving about in the public. If not, then we may not be looking for someone inside at all."

Carlo had been sitting with his face in his hands, and looked up and Sam for just a moment. He spread his hands as if in desperation, and then lowered his face back into them. "I know everyone in the prefecture and the papal family," he said. "I cannot imagine any of them who would harm His Holiness. The very concept would be anathema."

Spencer picked up his cup and took a sip of the strong, Italian coffee. "He's right," he said. "Just to imagine someone being within the papal family who could harm the pope, that's just not conceivable. These people are vetted more thoroughly than any candidate for a Supreme Court justice. I mean, look at Carlo. He's almost 70, now, and I think the youngest person in the prefecture is probably a nun in her 50s. You get into the papal family by being chosen after a fairly long life of devotion to the church. These people are known for their piety, not for any kind of greed or desire for power."

Indie shrugged. "Pious people make mistakes, too," she said. "Chandler was into blackmail, not just bribery. If he found something on someone in there that they didn't want exposed, it wouldn't be that hard to convince them to do what he wanted in order to avoid that exposure."

"That's very true," Sam said. "That's one of the reasons that so many people in governments all over the world were afraid of him, and won't step up to prevent his plans from going into action, even though he's dead now. We're not sure if he had some sort of organization in place that would expose the information he used to force cooperation, or if it's some kind of automated device or system that will send that information out if certain conditions are not met. All we know is that even other governments are afraid to interfere in this situation."

Spencer looked Sam in the eye. "Then, I'm going to ask you a point-blank question. What makes you so determined to stop it, if even the government hasn't taken a stance against it? What makes you more certain of your position than they are of theirs?"

Sam gave him a shark toothed smile. "I give you a point-blank answer," he said. "What makes me more certain of my position is knowing that there's no way in the world I could sleep at night if I allow these things to happen. Look, Chandler was following some weird old religion that was all about taking over the world and forcing your will upon it. Or, his will, in this case. I don't know where you stand on religion, though your position makes me think that you have at least some confidence in the Christian perspective, am I right?"

"You're absolutely right," Spencer said with a smile of his own. "I served the church long before I served the government, and my loyalties haven't changed."

Sam nodded. "Okay, then that being the case, I have to point at biblical prophecy. From everything I've been told, there are certain things that have to happen before the rise of the Antichrist. Since those things haven't happened, Chandler was trying to create his own version of the end times, rather than follow the script that God laid out. If you take all of that into consideration, then there's no way that we can even speculate that Chandler's plan should go forward. The fact that our governments are refusing to take action only speaks of their cowardice, not of the rightness of any plan Chandler came up with."

Carlo dropped his hands to the tabletop.

"Gentlemen," he said, "oh, and my dear lady, let me remind you that we are still talking about some of the most horrific things that man has ever conceived. His Holiness would willingly lay down his own life to prevent these other atrocities; I know him. The problem is that, in this situation, what we have to do is stop that from happening. We must find a way to stop this assassination, to stop the person behind it. But how do we stop them, when we have no clue who they are?"

Sam looked at the old priest. "Father, let me ask you this," he said. "What will be the pope's response if we tell him about this plot? Would he cooperate with us in our efforts to keep him alive?"

"Oh, I'm certain he would," Carlo said, grinning. "As holy as he is, there is that part of him which is still human and does not wish to die. If we said to him that his death would serve a great purpose, he would not hesitate to walk into the jaws of death itself, but since this case is precisely the opposite, and his death will trigger even greater tragedies, he will certainly want to do whatever it takes to prevent that."

"Then how do we get to him?" Sam asked. "I think we need to speak with him directly, if possible."

Carlo shook his head. "That will be a problem," he said. "I cannot take anyone into the papal apartments when His Holiness is sequestered, this way. The Swiss Guard have to approve every visitor, and will not accept any applications at this time." He looked at Spencer.

"Perhaps, John, you can make some arrangement?"

"I can try," Spencer said. "Carlo is right, in that the Swiss Guard is declining applications for an audience with His Holiness during his voluntary sequestration. However, I know a few of the officers and might be able to get one to issue a summary approval. If that doesn't work, I can go to the ambassador, but I have no way of knowing whether he might be involved in this plot, himself. My office chief warned me to keep my nose out of it, when I tried to find out who picked up an unusual package the other day, and since he's never spoken to me that way before, I have to wonder if perhaps Chandler got to him. If the ambassador is also involved, I could be putting my life on the line just to ask the question."

Sam nodded, and glanced at Indie before he answered. "Spencer, you're right," he said. "You could very well be putting your life at risk. What you got to remember, though, is that the whole world is at risk if we don't find a way to stop this assassination. If there were a way I can take that risk upon myself for you, I would be glad to do that, but at the moment it seems like you're the man."

Spencer laughed, and reached over to gently punch Sam in the arm. "Well, as a matter of fact," he said, "it just occurred to me that we might be smarter to let me introduce you to the ambassador, so that you can bring up the idea of getting to His Holiness. I got a hunch that you'd know pretty quickly if the ambassador is involved, and I'd be willing to do whatever I can to get you out if that were the case."

Indie reached across the table to put her hand onto Sam's. "Babe," she said, "if you go in there, I'm going with you."

Sam winked at her, not a bit surprised at her determination, but even less inclined to go along with her decision. On the other hand, their current setting was not the place to discuss it, so he didn't say anything to her in response. He looked again at Spencer.

"Okay, so first, you're going to try talking to these Swiss Guard officers, right?"

Spencer nodded. "Yes, sir, that's what I've got in mind."

Sam nodded. "All right, then," he said. "If you're successful, we'll know it because of that unmentionable wiretap we didn't discuss earlier. If you need to get hold of us for any reason, all you got to do is pick up your phone and start talking into it. We got it set so that we hear pretty much everything that goes through it. In fact, when you go in to talk to your boss about this, be sure to keep it on in your pocket. That way, we'll hear everything that goes on and we can even record it."

"Well, that sounds good, anyway. It's nice to know somebody's got my back."

Sam nodded. "Yeah," he said, "I know exactly how you feel on that. Now, we've got to get moving on this, right away. We don't know what our deadline is, what possible scenarios may already be playing out. How soon can you get a response back from those officers?"

Spencer looked at his cup for a moment, and then back up at Sam. "Well," he said, "I really don't want to try doing that over the phone. The smart move would be for me to go and visit them face-to-face, don't you think?"

"Yeah, I'd say that would be best. I hate to say it, but if it's that easy for us to put a tap on you, it's probably just as easy for anyone else who wanted to. So I'll amend my question, how long before you can get to them and get their response, then relay that response back to us?"

Spencer shrugged. "If I leave right now, I could probably talk to them within the next thirty minutes. There are only two that I really need to check with, and luckily they're both in the same office. If I can catch them together, we can be finished in a matter of minutes. They'll either say yea or nay, it's about that simple. Give me a number, and I can call you directly. All I'd have to say is something simple and harmless, like if I say that I'm really enjoying the weather, it means for you to come on, you're in."

Sam grinned, then took out a pen and scribbled his number onto a slip of paper, which he passed to Spencer. "The sooner you can get moving on this, the better. I'd suggest you go now. That'll give us and Carlo the chance to get to know each other better, right,

Carlo?"

The old priest looked up at Sam with a nervous smile on his face. "Mr. Prichard," he said, his Italian accent adding a syllable here and there. "Please don't think that I am not willing to do anything I can to aid you in protecting our pontiff, but to be honest, this is all extremely overwhelming for a man of my years. How can I know, for instance, that you are who you say you are? How am I to know whether to trust you, or to keep you as far from His Holiness as I possibly can?" He clasped his hands together in front of his face and closed his eyes, and it was obvious that the movement of his lips was the subvocalization of a silent prayer. He continued silently for a full minute, as Spencer rose to leave, nodding to Sam and Indie as he departed. A moment later, Carlo finally opened his eyes, but he turned them to Indie rather than to Sam.

The old man's eyes bored into the young woman's, and she was slightly taken aback for just a moment. That didn't last long, however, because Indie was a strong young woman who had already been through a lot in her short life. She smiled at the old man and then reached over and put her hand on top of one of his.

"My dear young lady," Carlos said to her, "it is as I pray that I believe God has shown me that there is a truth within you, a truth that is greater than that within your husband. This is not to say that he is not an honest man, only that he has lived and worked in situations that have required him to be able to dissemble when necessary. You, I sense, are a woman full of love, and full of hope and happiness. We know, from the thirteenth chapter of the first epistle to the Corinthians, that love is the greatest of all of the virtues. Love never fails. Though everything else may pass away, love never fails." Carlo put his left hand over the one Indie had laid on his right. "And so it is that I must ask you, is this all true? Is it you and your husband, and those with you, whom I should trust?"

The old man's eyes never left Indie's, not even for a second. She smiled and looked as directly into them as she could. "Father Carlo," she began, "this is the first time I have ever had to work with Sam on one of these missions, but if there's one thing I know for certain, it's that he is the most honest, trustworthy, loyal man that has ever lived. I left our daughter at home in America to come and help him here, because I know that what he is doing is the right thing to do. Yes, you can trust us, because we want the same thing that you do. We want to stop these things from happening, all of them, from this first attempt to assassinate the pope, all the way through to each of the most horrendous things this evil man dreamed up."

Carlos smiled back. "Do you know," he asked, "that there was a time when, despite everything the Bible taught me, I honestly believed that evil was nothing more than the selfishness of man. The whole concept of a personal devil, of a Satan who was an individual spirit that actively sought to destroy what God hath built, that concept was so foreign to me. Satan would've been part of God's creation, yes? How, then, could he have turned against his father, his creator, how could he seek to destroy the very race of mankind that God created to be his children?" The old man closed his eyes for a moment and raised his face toward the ceiling, as if looking through it with spiritual eyes that allowed him to see directly into heaven. A soft smile crept across his lips, and Indie found herself staring at him and wonder. "And so, I prayed for God to give me understanding, to help me to discern the spirit of evil, and do you know how He responded? God raised me up from where I served as the pastor of a very small church, and brought me to Rome. He installed me in the Vatican, and made me a helper and a student of all those who serve His Holiness, who strive to teach and interpret the Word and Will of God unto the church. In this place, where Holiness should abound and fill every corner, every little space, I have learned more about evil than in all the rest of my life, and in all of the places I have seen. Greed, jealousies, envy, falsehoods, even lusts have I seen among all of these Holy Brethren and the Holy Sisters who serve alongside them."

Indie shrugged, then kept smiling at the old man. "I guess people are the same, no matter where you go. We're all human, and we all make mistakes, right? I think that a lot of what we think of as evil is really just a matter of people not understanding what it is they should do, not really being sure how to do it. For the most part, that doesn't mean that they're bad people, it just means they're human. But then, of course, you run across people like Chandler, people who are so evil that they don't care who they hurt or how badly, as long as they get what they want. That's all that matters to them, getting their way, getting everything to go the way they wanted to go."

Sam leaned toward Carlo. "I can understand what you're saying," he said. "I understand what Indie has been saying, too, that most of the time it isn't about real evil as much as it's about people just being selfish and greedy. That goes along with what you said, what you originally thought evil was. The thing is, it's become clear to me lately that there really is such a thing as pure evil, and while I may never have quite believed some of the Bible stories about demons being cast out, I can tell you that if I have ever in my life come face-to-face with a man who was possessed, it was Chandler. When I got the word that he was dead, as terrible as this sounds, I felt nothing but relief. The world is simply better off without him in it."

Carlo had turned to look at Sam. "Indeed, I do understand. I do agree. I will put my trust in you, and I will pray to my Father in Heaven that he will lead you and guide you." The old man rose to his feet. "I shall go now, and begin doing what I can do to find any clue that may help you. May God lead me to the person behind this awful plan, so that you may stop him from doing his deed, and thereby prevent even worse things from happening. You shall be in my prayers, both of you and all those with you."

Carlo turned and walked away, leaving the little pizzeria with his head held high. Sam looked at his wife. "Think we ought to grab some pizza, take it back to the hotel with us? We may be sitting around for a while."

Indie shook her head. "Those guys can get something to eat if they get hungry," she said. "I've got a hunch that you're going to be hearing from Spencer pretty quickly, and we're closer to him here than we would be back at the hotel. If you're hungry now, then let's get something to eat, but I'm not." She held up her glass and grinned at him. "But you could get me another glass of *Chinotto.*"

Sam took her glass and smiled, then rose and went to the little counter to get it refilled.

There were so many things going through his mind that he found himself wondering just how real this whole situation could be. Ancient prophecies, he was sitting in Rome, just outside the Vatican, talking with officials from inside the Holy See – the whole thing felt like he'd been caught up in a Dan Brown novel, but too many things had happened for him to believe that it was all in his imagination. When Indie's glass had been refilled, he carried it back to the booth and sat down across from her again.

"I'm going to check in with Harry, real quick," he

said, taking his phone out of his pocket.

"Okay," Indie said. "Tell the old goat I said hello."

Sam punched the Elmer Fudd button on his phone, and waited for a moment while the international connection went through. Harry was still in the hospital in Jerusalem, of course, but Sam had hadn't spoken to him since he and Ken had left Israel.

"Sam? Is it you?"

"Harry, come on, now, who else would be calling you on my phone?" Sam asked with a laugh. "Just wanted to check in, let you know that we've made contact with some people in the Vatican and we're working on getting a lead on who we need to locate there."

"Good, good," the old man said. "I gather you've heard the news? About Chandler?"

"Yeah, Natasha called me yesterday as we were waiting for the plane to take off. Ken and I have been trying to figure out who the 'she' might be that he's referring to. Gary thinks it could be Sandra, but I'm not so sure."

Sandra Ross, the current Secretary of State, is a highly manipulative and dangerous individual, and has been making a bid to become president of the United States one day. The mere thought of this was terrifying.

"This whole damn thing is so convoluted," Harry said, "that I wouldn't be all that surprised to find my own mother involved in it somewhere."

"Well, I just wanted to bring you up to date. Indie

and I had an interesting meeting with a man from the office of the embassy to the Vatican, and an old priest who works in the pope's own household. Between the two, were hoping to get a lead on how Chandler's assassination plan was supposed to play out.

"Excellent! What's your plan of attack when you find out who to tackle there in Vatican City?"

"Well, my first step will probably be to try to reason with them, but that hasn't worked on anyone connected to it so far, has it? Harry, I don't want to kill anybody, if I can avoid it, but I'll be blunt and honest. If it's the only way to stop this plan from coming off, then I'll do what I have to do. Ken is all set, I think he's just waiting for me to turn him loose on somebody."

"Well, that's kind of understandable," Harry said, "when you consider that he has devoted his entire life to protecting this country by doing the jobs nobody else wants to do. To him, this is just the way you handle things, and it's probably chafing at him a bit that he has to let you hold the reins. Of course, that's one of the reasons I wanted you in charge, too."

"Gee, thanks, Harry," Sam said, sneering into the phone. "By the way, Indie said to tell you hello. When we get to figuring out what this is going to cost Uncle Sam, I think another expense paid trip to Europe might be in order. One we can use as a vacation, and be real tourists and sightseers for once."

"Sam, you pull this off and I'll pay for it out of my

own pocket if I have to! Hell, I might even pack up and come with you! Or would I be too much of a damper on your good spirits?"

Sam put the phone on speaker and looked at Indie. "Harry wants to know if he could come with us on a vacation to Europe, or if he put too much of a damper on us."

Indie smiled, and took the phone from Sam's hand. "Harry? You old buzzard, if you want to take a trip with us, you're more than welcome. Just don't get all jealous and upset when I lock you out of the room now and then, so I can have Sam all to myself."

Harry laughed heartily, and then groaned a couple of times when the laughing made him hurt. "I don't think there would be any problem there," he said. "I think I can understand you kids wanting some privacy, now and then. I vaguely recall certain things about my younger days that might explain why you'd want them."

Indie laughed. "Harry, you're not fooling anyone," she said. "I'm pretty sure those memories aren't that far back. And if they are, then all you got to do is flirt with my mom or Grace a little bit—they both got the hots for you."

"Okay, you're embarrassing me, now," Harry said, but there was a chuckle in his voice. "Sam, I appreciate you keeping me up-to-date. If you need anything, and I mean anything at all, don't you hesitate to call. Doesn't matter what time of day or night, if you call, I'm going to answer." The line went dead, the way it always did when Harry was finished talking on the phone.

Sam put the phone down on the table, and smiled at his wife. "Could be nice," he said, "if we managed to wrangle ourselves a European vacation at Uncle Sam's expense."

Indie reached across to hold hands with Sam. "Sam," she said, seductively, "you don't really think Harry would try to come along with us, do you?"

Sam laughed. "Well, if he does, then we have to bring Kenzie along, too. The two of them can babysit each other."

"Hmpf," Indie said. "That would be a tossup on which one of them was really in charge."

"No it wouldn't," Sam said. "Kenzie would have Harry wrapped around her little finger in about eight seconds flat, and he'd be doing her bidding for the rest of the trip. The old man would probably spend most of his retirement savings just buying her all the goodies she wanted."

They were both startled, suddenly, when Sam's phone rang again. He glanced at it, but didn't know the number. It was a local cell number, so he answered it quickly.

"Prichard," he said.

"Mr. Prichard, it's John Spencer. I spoke with my two friends, and they've agreed to arrange for me to meet with His Holiness. I asked about bringing you with me, and they said they preferred that I speak to him alone at first. If he wants to meet with you, then they'll arrange it. I'll be meeting with him in about ten minutes. Sir, is there anything in particular you want me to say to him?"

"Well, we don't have any idea whether he knows who Chandler was, right? Assuming that he didn't, then I guess the best thing to do is simply try to explain to him what Chandler was up to. Spencer, do you feel like you understand it enough to explain it to the pope?"

"I've got the gist of it, sir," Spencer said. "I think I can make him understand the general plot, and that seems to be the important part, don't you think? He needs to know that this whole convoluted plan involves everything from replacing him with some puppet of Chandler's, and from that, triggering a whole plethora of other troubles and disasters."

"Yeah, that pretty much covers it. All right, how soon do you think you can let me know what happens?"

"Oh, I'd say you'll know pretty shortly. They're waving at me to come on, now, so I've got to get off the phone. I'll call you back as soon as I possibly can. Later, dude." The line went dead.

Sam looked at Indie. "Well, you are partly right," he said. "Spencer is on his way in to see the pope, right now. Hopefully, will have some response back from him pretty soon."

Indie suddenly shivered, and looked at Sam. "Do you ever wonder," she asked, "if maybe we've actually stepped into some twilight zone kind of thing, where devils romp around and prophecies come true?"

Sam shrugged. "Baby," he said. "I think we were all born there." He sat there and held her hand in silence for a few minutes.

After ten minutes had passed, Sam suddenly couldn't sit still anymore, and got up, pulling Indie along with him. Holding her hand, he led her out the front door of the restaurant and they began walking down the street.

"Sam?" Indie asked. "Where are we going?"

Sam glanced at her, and for some reason she felt a chill run down her spine. "I just felt like we had to get out of there," he said. "I just couldn't sit there anymore, waiting. This whole thing could start at any moment, and we have no idea how to stop it. It's driving me up a wall, it's driving me crazy."

Indie looked at her husband, and her heart went out to him. "I know," she said. "It's getting to me, too. I feel like I'm sitting here twiddling my thumbs, wasting time, when I should be out doing something. I wonder if I should be sitting back at the hotel, working with Gary on the computers, but he's so far beyond me, I don't know what I can do to be of help. I feel better, just being here with you. Is that selfish?"

Sam shrugged, but he smiled at her. "If it is, then we're both being selfish. I feel better, too, having you with me. I don't think I want to be tackling this without you, not right now."

Sam's phone rang, and he pulled it out to see the same number he'd seen before. "It's Prichard," he said.

"Mr. Prichard," came Spencer's voice. "I am sitting here with His Holiness, the pope. I've explained what's going on, and he has asked me to express to you his gratitude for your efforts to preserve his life. He has asked the Commandant of the Swiss Guard to immediately secure the papal apartments, so that no one inside can leave, and of course, no one outside can come in. Every person who is employed in any capacity that allows them to get near the pontiff is being systematically rounded up at this moment, and a full investigation is being launched. Now, the idea isn't so much to catch the perpetrator, though, as to see who tries to take off. As it happens, the Commandant has special authority and connections with Italian government authorities, so it's highly unlikely that anyone on that list could get very far. All forms of public transportation are being put on restriction immediately, so that every passenger must produce identification and be checked against the list of names and photographs, all done through facial recognition computers when ever they go to buy a ticket.. In addition, no one can drive out of the country without going through a checkpoint. I suspect we'll have some idea of who it is we're looking for within the next hour, and the Commandant has arranged for any suspects to be made available to you for questioning."

Sam's eyes were wide, and he whistled. "Holy cow,"

he said, "Spencer, that's incredible. Great job!"

"Aww, shucks, partner, I didn't do nothing!" Spencer said. "Seriously, sir, all I did was tell His Holiness what you told me, and he did the rest with a phone call. Oh, I hope it's okay, I did have to give your number to the Commandant. That's all right, isn't it?"

"Of course it is," Sam said. "Now, we just have to hope that we round up the right party."

9

With nothing left to do but wait, Sam and Indie decided to go back to the hotel. Ken and Gary were happy to see them, especially when they were brought up to date on the pope's response. Both men wanted to hear all the details, and as soon as Sam and Indie were done talking, it became obvious that Gary had just as much to say.

"So, okay, I've been doing a lot of digging," he said. "Remember, just before you left, we were speculating on who Chandler might have been referring to, in those cryptic last words of his. Well, I went on the assumption that it would be someone easily recognizable to the American public, but also to the rest of the world, and that it would be someone that at least a fair number of people would regard as a potential world leader. Now, if we add in the fact that it has to be a woman, it don't matter how you try to slice it, you're only going to come up with one name. Now, I realize that we're all sick and tired of conspiracy theories, but if you go back through all of Chandler's personal files and notes, an awful lot of the things they said about Mrs. Ross have at least some basis in truth. You are aware, aren't you, that she's been accused many times of being the antichrist? Well, try this on for size. Back when she was first lady, there was a rumor that went around that she decorated a Christmas tree with some..." Gary glanced at Indie, and turned a bit pinkish before going on. "Well, that she used condoms and little male figures who were, um, let's just say they were obviously very male, that's the rumor that went around. But I got to poking around in some of Chandler's personal files that I copied from the office network, and I found a couple of amazing photographs of a tree decorated exactly that way, and would you like to guess who's in those photos? That doesn't really have much to do with this situation, but if you're looking at the overall picture, it shows some pretty strange vibes, wouldn't you think?"

Sam rolled his eyes. "Pretty strange, yeah, I'll go along with that," he said. "But what does any of this have to do with Chandler? Or any kind of connection between them?"

Gary grinned and nodded, his glasses bobbing up and down on his nose. "I was getting to that," he said, "don't be so impatient! I can show you about three dozen different files that connect Sandra to an organization called the Muslim Sisterhood, and a number of documents showing that she deliberately arranged for certain Christian organizations to be stifled while at the same time, and very publicly, she was promoting tolerance and acceptance of Muslim principles. She and her top aide, Huma Abedin, both members of the Muslim Sisterhood, are apparently pretty close to other members, who include the wives of high-ranking officials in many Muslim countries. Man, this lady has Chandler written all over her!"

Ken shook his head at Sam. "Don't let yourself get excited," he said. "Don't get me wrong, I'd love to pin this on her, but I have my doubts. I mean, first off, if she were really the one Chandler was grooming for all of this, I can't believe he would've let all these rumors go crazy. He could pick up the phone and make anyone disappear, anywhere in the world, and we know that to be a fact. That being the case, I just can't see him allowing all of those rumors to fly around Sandra if he really had any inclination towards using her in his plans. And frankly, I can't see why in the world he'd want to use her. I mean, after what happened in Benghazi and so many other screwed up situations, and then the whole thing about her having some blood clot in the brain – I don't know, but to me, all of those things would make her 'hands off,' if I were the one making those decisions."

"Then, you're not swallowing any of this, this whole concept that she's the one Chandler wanted to put in place? I don't know, I've got to admit that from what little

I know, she almost seems like the ideal candidate. And let's face it, she's got the political clout. There are still people who think she'd make a great president."

Indie shuddered. "Oh, Lord, I hope not in my lifetime, or my daughter's!"

Sam laughed at her. "Baby, I'm in complete agreement," he said. "The thing is, none of this is getting us any closer to figuring out what to do next." He looked at Gary. "Now you're getting a taste of what real investigation and fieldwork is like," he said. "It's mostly just sitting around and waiting, hoping to get the next clue in time to do something with it."

"Oh, I understand that," Gary said. "I had to go through every debriefing report, every after action report, every analysis report – some days I thought my eyes were going to fall out from staring at the monitor." He looked at Indie. "You ready to get to work? You can set up on the other side of this table, and we can coordinate our searches so that we're covering twice as much data."

Indie smiled. "Sure, glad to. I feel like I'm just in the way, standing around here like this. Give me a minute." She grabbed her laptop case and got it out, and had it set up a moment later. Gary gave her the log-on instructions for the super Wi-Fi the government kept at the Royal Palace Hotel. Moments later, she had her computer live and running. "Okay," she said, "where do you want me to start?"

Gary grinned. "I'm sending you some links; these are pages online that are secretly connected to Chandler's plans. You'll be going in through a proxy I've set up, so you won't need all the passwords for each site; what I want you to do is search them for anything you think might give us any idea of what to do next. Turn Herman loose, and see what he can find, y'know?"

"Okay," she said, "I see them. So I'm running through your computer to get to these pages?"

"Yep," Gary said. "I'm already logged in, so by running through the proxy in my system you don't have to worry about logging in to each and every one of them. Using those links, Herman can go in and scan all of the pages without any problem."

Indie smiled. "Sweet! I'm on it!"

Sam sat down beside Indie, and the two of them started discussing search parameters for Indie to feed into Herman. That meant that, since she had already given him the links to search, they needed to tell him what to look for.

"This Mesopotamian God that Chandler seemed to worship was called Shamash. Let's look for any reference to him, especially to any prophecies concerning him. That would give us at least something to start with. Then, let's look for any reference to Mrs. Ross. If he's honestly got her in his plan to be the figurehead, then we ought to be able to find some mention of her, somewhere."

Indie nodded. "Yes, but the more I think about it,

the less I believe it. He would want someone believable in that position, someone reliable. She said so many gaffes that it's just beyond comprehension to think that anyone would accept her as the new world leader."

Sam shrugged, but looked her in the eye. "Really? If you studied your history, you know there was a time when a fair number were prepared to accept a man like Adolf Hitler. You'd be surprised what people will accept, when they think it will make life easier for them. I always got a kick out of psychology professors, with their references to prime motivations. In my experience, the prime motivation of mankind is always nothing more than, 'Me! Me!' People want what makes their own lives as easy as possible, and they don't really give a rip how it may affect anyone else. If she steps up after the disasters Chandler planned, then yeah, I could see the world accepting her. You got to remember that we live in a very sick society."

Indie made a face. "Yeah, I know," she said. "Still, makes you wonder how sick it could be." She tapped her keys, giving Herman his instructions and then turning him loose to do his thing. The program almost instantly started *dinging* to tell her it had found something, and even Indie looked surprised. She glanced at both Sam and Gary before she clicked on the first link to appear. It was in a page of Chandler's notes, apparently, like a journal he was keeping. Indie read it aloud, so that they could all hear it at once.

"M has no idea just how important she is to the

*whole plan, but I'm sure she is the one Shamash refers
to in the ninth line of the twenty second prophecy: "The
woman of power is made first among my councils, and is
given the place of leadership, for my hand shall be
hidden, I say, behind her veils." As far as I can tell, this
means that the world's new leader is to be female, and
won't that be a shock to all those Muslims. Shamash
wants his real power, which is me, to be concealed. I'm
to be the real ruler, while M takes the credit and gets the
praise. No wonder I've always been the one to work
behind the scenes. That was always Shamash, preparing
me for the most important role I would have to play."*

Indie read the passage again, as Sam and Ken looked
at each other. "Who is 'M?'" Sam asked. "That's the
question we have to answer."

Ken nodded. "Yeah, but at least we do know we're
looking for a woman. Just having that confirmed is a
pretty big plus, right now."

"Yeah, I have to agree," said Sam. He turned back
to Indie. "Now the question is, how to identify that
woman. If it is Sandra, I still say there should be some
reference to her, somewhere. If it's not, then we ought to
be finding something to indicate who it is."

"Herman's still looking," Indie said. "We gotta give
him time. Be patient, baby, he'll come up with
something. Doesn't he always?"

There had been a few more chimes while the

reading and talking was going on, and Indie turned back to the computer to see what they were. She clicked on the first link in the list, and found another page of notes. She scanned through them quickly, but didn't find anything that told them anything new, so she skipped on to the next one. This one looked like a page with links to other websites, and for a moment she got excited. When she clicked the first of the links on the page, it went to a news story about the Benghazi incident, a story that pointed out how Sandra Ross had avoided repeated orders to testify about what happened there. Seeing that, Indie thought she might be onto evidence that Mrs. Ross was the M they were looking for, but when she clicked the next link she found a story about a train derailleur derailment in India, and then the next one was about an election in an African country. None of them seemed to be related at all to Chandler's plans, but then it suddenly hit her.

"Sam!" Indie said. "Look at this!" She pointed out the reference to Benghazi, then the train derailleur and the election, which the article indicated had not gone the way the people expected to go. The next article after that one was about the death of an ambassador from Nigeria, and the one after that detailed the bombing of a US military installation in Afghanistan.

Sam looked, read through the articles as she showed them to him, but then just looked at her. "Babe," he said, "I don't get it. What do all these things have to do with Chandler's plot, or with finding out who M is?"

Indie grinned. "I didn't get it at first, either," she said. "We told Herman to find things that were related to Chandler's plans, and that's exactly what he did. The trouble was that we were thinking of things he was planning that were yet to come, while Herman put two and two together and figured out that all of these were parts of his plot, as well. The death of our ambassador in Benghazi? A train goes off the rails in India? Take a good look, in every single one of these incidents, someone powerful is eliminated. In Benghazi, the US ambassador died, and was, of course, replaced by someone else when the time came. In India, when that train went off the tracks, over a hundred people died, and three of them were government officials. If you catch the footnote on that story, they were the three who were opposing India's leadership, on some new governmental reforms. The Nigerian ambassador to Egypt is assassinated, and a week later there are some new agreements between those two countries that nobody thought were possible under the old guy. Sam, all of these are things Chandler arranged, every single one of them."

"She's right," Gary said, and Ken echoed him a second later. "That's exactly what he did, he arranged things like these in order to create vacancies that allowed him to put puppets of his own into place. I'll be honest, it never even occurred to me that Benghazi could have been one of his, but when I look at it now, it's pretty obvious."

"Ironic, isn't it?" Ken asked. "I was using Benghazi to justify why I didn't believe he'd want to use her, and now it turns out that she was basically just holding the bag for him on that one. Sort of looks like he stuck it to her, doesn't it?"

Sam nodded. "It does, but it doesn't necessarily eliminate her as a candidate, either. We don't know what arrangement might have been made on that, or how it might conceivably have benefited her."

Indie crinkled her eyes at him. "Benefited her?" She asked. "Sam, she got raked over the coals on that one. I don't think there was much benefit to her in it, anywhere. I'm not defending her, don't get me wrong, but I can remember all that stuff on CNN about how the senators and congressmen were screaming for her blood over that."

"Yeah, I remember that too," he said, "but it's quite possible that was nothing but camouflage. They may have wanted that big fuss, just to keep anyone from speculating on what have been behind that event. Since everyone was looking at Sandra, screaming that she should have done something or somehow prevented that tragedy, no one was paying any attention to whoever it was that stood to gain from it. Maybe we should be looking at that."

Ken shook his head. "I don't think so," he said. "Just the very fact that not one of us can think of who took over after Chris Stevens was killed says it's probably not that great a connection. It was passed off as a terrorist act, an attack by terrorists against the United States. Stevens and the others who died were supposedly just collateral damage, but now that we know Chandler was involved, then we know that someone stood to gain something, and probably from the fact that Stevens died."

"Laurence Pope," Gary said, staring at his monitor. "He was appointed as ambassador to Libya in October 2012, about a month after Stevens was killed. Anybody want to take a guess who was behind his appointment?"

"Oh, let's see," Sam said, "would that be Sandra Ross?"

"Nope!" Gary said. "The suggestion for the appointment came from none other than Grayson Chandler, who is listed as an advisor to the president on matters related to diplomatic relations with Muslim nations. On the other hand, Mr. Pope had retired back in two thousand, and had to come out of retirement to fill that slot. His entire career in the diplomatic corps is about as exemplary as it could get. I mean, this guy has never had a blemish of any kind on his record, not even the slightest little black mark. He's about as clean as a man can get, and at seventy years old, he's pretty well retired, again, now. I can't find anything to indicate a connection to Chandler, no real benefit that he might've gained from Stevens' death."

Sam leaned back in his chair and rubbed his eyes.

"So we're back to square one," he said. "Seems like this whole thing is twisted around in so many directions that is almost impossible to figure out where any part of it could be going."

"Well, if you were Chandler, isn't that the way you'd want it?" Indie asked. "Let's face it, nobody would want their plan to take over the world to be completely obvious to everyone, would they? If you were doing it, wouldn't you build it in such a way that every clue someone thought they found simply led them down another dead-end road?"

"I guess I'd try," Sam said. "On the other hand, how hard would it be to anticipate every possible attempt to figure out what you're doing and throw roadblocks up in front of them? Any mind that could do that would be pretty frightening. I know I could never pull off something like that, and frankly, I don't think I know of any other human being who could."

Ken suddenly looked up at Sam. "A thought just ran through my head," he said. "Remember the other day, we were on the way to DC when Harry called. He said something that I thought was odd, he said that Chandler seemed to be scared that you were going to stop him. Remember that?"

Sam nodded. "Yeah, I remember."

Ken cocked his head to one side. "Here's what's bothering me," he said. "Up until you got involved with me, Chandler had never even heard of you. And yet, for some reason we don't know, as soon as he heard you were involved in my efforts to stop him, he started getting nervous. Now, why is that, I wonder? Anybody got any ideas?"

No one did. Gary turned to his computer and started tapping keys rapidly. "I'm telling Mad Maggie to run a search on any correlations between Chandler and Sam Prichard. Let's see if there's a connection somewhere that we're not aware of."

Gary turned his computer loose, while they all continue to watch what Herman was up to. Every few minutes there was another *ding* from Indie's computer, and they would all look to see what Herman had come up with next. There were links to more of Chandler's notes, but none of them gave any further indication of who the infamous M was, and there were links to more news stories about events that probably had Chandler's fingerprints all over them, but nothing that seemed to be useful. Time was passing, and everyone was getting uptight.

Suddenly, Mad Maggie signaled a result, and Gary spun his chair and rolled back to his side of the table. Everyone waited while he looked at what Maggie had reported, but when he gave a low whistle, they all hurried around to see for themselves.

"Okay," Gary said, "this is a page from a scholarly work on the prophecies of Shamash, from a Doctor Abdul Teresh, who actually interpreted some old

Mesopotamian tablets that were found about a hundred years ago. He was particularly interested in the prophecy of what he calls, 'the bright one,' which is the name that he gives to a prophesied figure whose purpose is to ferret out unworthy people in the high councils of Shamash. In other words, the bright one is supposed to be someone unknown, who comes out of nowhere, to defeat and destroy those who try to use their position for personal gain, rather than serving the true will of Shamash."

They all looked at one another, and then back at Gary. "So, what prompted the whistle?" Ken asked. "We all thought you were on to something."

"Yeah, well, don't sell me short," Gary said. "You're gonna freak when I read you the actual prophecy itself, are you ready? Here goes." He pointed at a section of text that was in italics on the screen. "And when my hand shall be stretched out to touch the whole earth, when that hand is prepared to hold all in its grasp, but shall drop into its brother a portion for itself, then shall my hand be false and full of sin. And there shall arise from the city on the mountain one to throw down my hand, and to punish and destroy my false hand, and his name shall be *Sam-per-shar*, he who shines."

There was nothing but silence in the room. Each of them looked at each other, but no one dared to speak. A minute passed, and then another, and finally it was Indie who broke the stillness with her voice.

"The city on the mountain? We live in Denver, the

mile high city in the Rocky Mountains. And the name, is anybody here going to say that it's just a coincidence? Sam Prichard — Sam-per-shar?"

Ken was shaking his head back and forth. "Well, I think we can see what it was about you that shook him up. If he truly studied those prophecies, then somewhere along the line he would've seen this one. Knowing you were from Denver, and having a name so close to the one in this prophecy? Hell, man, that would send chills down my spine if I were him."

Sam shrugged. "One of the things we been going on all this time is that none of the prophecies of Shamash had shown any sign of coming true, so I'm not going to go putting a lot of stock into this one, no matter how it looks. As far as I'm concerned, the only thing about me that should've scared Chandler was the fact that he was messing with my country. This isn't helping. This isn't giving us anything we need to figure out how to stop everything he put into motion. Let's get it done, come on — we've got to get some idea of who it is we're actually trying to stop."

Gary and Indie went back to work, letting their computers scan through thousands of pages of documents and websites in search of any information that might tell them what their next move should be. Even as good as the computers were, there was so much data to sift through that they knew it was going to take a while. Sam and Ken sat down and tried to think of new angles of their own, but they weren't having any luck.

Sam took out his phone and called Harry. The old man answered on the second ring, and Sam could hear the smile on his face through the line.

"Sam, boy, it's good to hear from you again. Where are we?"

Sam smiled back through the phone. "Hi, Harry," he said. "We're making a little progress, I think. The Pope has agreed to some heightened security measures, and they're rounding up just about everyone who could conceivably get to him right now. The Italian government has set up facial recognition, looking for any of his household employees who decide to try to flee the country. With any luck, we'll have some ideas soon of who it is we're looking for. At the very least, I think we've managed to put a kink into Chandler's plans."

"Glad to hear it," Harry said. "Every minute that goes by makes me worry that we've missed something important."

"Yeah, I know what you mean," Sam replied. "Hey, listen, remember a few days ago, you called and said how it almost seemed like Chandler was a little bit scared that I was going to get to him? Well, Gary ran across something interesting. There's an old prophecy of Shamash that actually says something about a man from the city on the mountain who would come to stop somebody who was trying to do what Shamash wanted, but for his own personal gain. Strangely enough, the name that prophecy gave to that person sounds a lot like my name."

Harry burst out laughing. "Now, wouldn't that be a kick in the pants? For him to see the person coming after him in the very prophecies he was trying to use to justify his own actions. That's amazing, Sam."

Sam chuckled along with him. "Yeah, I kinda thought you'd get a kick out of that. So how are you doing? Everything going okay there?"

"Oh, I'm fine. I'm driving the nurses here crazy, because they seem to have this wild notion that I'm going to do things their way, rather than the way I want to do them. I can't imagine how they could be that silly, but they are. And here comes one of them, right now, who seems to be under the impression that she's about to give me a bath. And do you know what? I think this is once when I just might be cooperative. You let me know if you need anything, Sam, boy, but I'm gonna have to go for now." The line went dead.

Sam laughed, and then had to explain to everyone what was so funny. All three of the others got a chuckle out of it, but then they got back to work. Gary found a few more prophetic references to the bright one, but nothing is clear as the first. Indie kept coming up with more and more items that appeared to be Chandler's handiwork, but still wasn't getting any closer to knowing who the infamous M could be. They were all getting impatient, but nothing seemed to be going in their favor.

And then Sam's phone rang. He picked it up to see

Spencer's number, and answered quickly.

"Prichard," he said.

"Sam, I think we've got something," Spencer said rapidly. "The Commandant just got a call from Rome's chief of police, and they have someone in custody right now. It's a man who has been a part of the Prefecture for more than a dozen years, but the moment the roundup was announced, he left like his tail was on fire. Went straight to the airport and tried to buy a ticket to New York City, but he was picked up and brought in for questioning. The Commandant suggested we turn him over to you, first. They have him at the Questura Centrale. That's the main police station, their headquarters. You can go there and ask for the *Capo della Polizia*. Just tell them your name, they know who you are."

"That's great, John," Sam said. "What's this fellow's name? The one they picked up?"

"Oh, right," Spencer said. "Just a second, I've got it here. Okay, here it is. His name is Harold Slater. He was an American priest, spent more than forty years as a priest in Albany, New York. Came here back in oh-three and has been working in the Vatican in one position or another, ever since."Sam scribbled down all of the information Spencer had given him. "Okay, thanks, John, I'm on it."

He quickly told the others what Spencer had said, then looked at Ken. "Let's go," he said. "I'll be good cop, you can be bad."

Ken grinned and got to his feet. "Let's do it!" he said.

10

Sam and Ken made it downstairs and to the paid parking lot where they kept the car in just a few minutes, and Sam let Ken drive since he was much more familiar with the city.

"I'm frankly surprised that the capo is going to even let you near the suspect, let alone question him," Ken said. "They're not usually that open to joint investigations, especially with the US. The only thing I can figure is that they don't want to piss off His Holiness."

Sam grinned. "Yeah, probably not. I would imagine it gets a little nerve-racking, having God's right-hand man sitting right in your lap, all the time. I can imagine they're a little cautious about getting him riled up."

"Well, I certainly would be. Don't get me wrong—personally, I don't think the Catholics have figured out that they're not exactly following Christian teaching. It flat amazes me that so many people could go to a church and read the Bible, and never quite notice that a lot of what they're being taught is in direct contradiction to what the scriptures say, but then, I've never been a Catholic, so maybe there are things about it I'm not seeing. I can't say I know everything, so maybe somebody else does."

Sam shrugged. "I'm pretty sure I don't. I know what I believe and that's good enough for me, but I don't claim to have any answers for anyone else. All I want to do is get this case over with, and then go home and retire, again. I've got a band back home that's just hoping I get back in time for the next gig we've got planned, at some new place that's opening up. Just think, when I get back to the microphone, I may just decide never to stop singing again!"

"Hmph. Probably the smartest move you make. Get as far away from this racket as you possibly can."

"Yeah," Sam said. "I'd be lying if I didn't say I was ready. I've got a wife and little girl who need me, and I'd like to be around for them. One of my biggest fears, every time Harry's tapped me for one of these missions, is that I would die and never get to see them again."

"I understand that," Ken said. "I wish I had known my family, and able to be the father that Joellyn needed, but the truth is that I just couldn't have handled trying to balance the two lives. When I was recruited, they made it clear that the country needed me so badly that any sacrifice was worthwhile. I fell for that, hook, line and sinker. They had me, and I think they knew it." He glanced at Sam, then turned his eyes back to the road in front of them. "I'm not going to tell you your country doesn't need you, Sam, obviously it does. You've already saved it more than once, and here you are working on it again. What I am going to say, though, is that you aren't the only one who can do that. When this one is over, take your chance to get out. Walk away, don't look back, just say goodbye to Harry and everything that's part of his world. That's the best advice I can give you, and probably the best advice you've ever had in your life."

Sam sat there quietly as the car rolled through the streets of Rome. He looked around him at the incredible mixture of structures, some of them thousands of years old, some of them as new as last week. Rome was an amazing city, but Sam was wishing he had never seen it at all.

They pulled up at the questura, and found a place to park the car. They got out together and entered the building, asking a uniformed officer where to find the office of the capo. He gave them directions, and they found the office with no trouble.

An officer greeted them as they entered, and Sam said, "I was told to come here to question a suspect who may be involved in the plot to assassinate the pope. My name is Sam Prichard, and I am with United States Homeland Security."

The officer looked at him strangely, and then shrugged his shoulders. "I know nothing of any suspect who is trying to assassinate His Holiness. Are you sure you have come to the right place?"

Sam looked at Ken, who looked just as confused as he was. He turned back to the officer. "I was contacted by a man from our embassy to the Holy See, and he told me that you had a suspect in custody. A priest named Harold Slater. They told me to ask the chief of police, because I was supposed to interrogate this man."

"Just one moment," the officer said, and picked up the telephone. He spoke rapidly into it in Italian, glancing at Sam more than once as he did so. After a moment, he nodded into the telephone, then hung up and turned back to Sam. "I am sorry, Signore," he said. "We have no such suspect, and no such person by that name. I just asked our inspector general if we know anything about a plan to assassinate the pope, and he assures me that we do not. I wish I could help you, but I don't know where to turn."

Sam and Ken looked at each other again, and then Sam bolted out the door. Ken was right on his heels, and caught up with him by the time he got back to the ground floor and the front doors. They got to the car at the same time, and jumped inside. "Go, go, go!" Sam shouted. "It was a trick of some sort, to get us away from the room." He had his phone out and was already dialing Indie. The phone rang twice, and then she answered.

"Sam?" She started to say something more, but Sam cut her off.

"Grab Gary," he said hurriedly, "and get the two of you out of that room, right now! We were sent on a wild goose chase, you've got to get out of there, now!"

"We what? Oh, Sam, oh my God..."

"Hurry, babe, get out of there now! If you can get into another room, go there, if not then start down the stairs. Don't use the elevators, anybody coming up would be coming that way. Hurry, go—Ken and I will be there as fast as we can. Go to the bistro for now, we'll meet you there."

"Okay, we're going! What about the computers? Oh, never mind, we're leaving them. Come on, Gary, we've gotta go now! Sam, I love you and I'll call you when we get to the bistro." She hung up, and Sam knew she was probably dragging Gary away from his precious equipment.

The car was racing through the streets, and Ken was surprised that they hadn't picked up a police escort, with the way he was screeching around corners. It'd taken them almost fifteen minutes to get to the police station, but he was trying to cut it down to ten on the way back. He kept his foot down on the accelerator, and was amazing Sam with his ability to weave in and out of traffic, avoid hitting cars who had the right-of-way in every intersection they came to, and generally avoid killing them both as they raced back to the hotel.

They slid to a stop in front of the bistro, and Sam was out of the car in a split second. He dashed inside, but there was no sign of Indie or Gary, so he spun and rushed out again. They ran into the hotel together, and Sam began rushing up the stairs while Ken took the elevator. The elevator was old and rather slow, so they actually got to their room at the same time.

The door was open, and there was no sign of either Gary or Indie inside. There was, however, a woman sitting at the table where the computers were set up. She turned to face them as they entered, and they saw the gun in her hand instantly.

"Hello, gentlemen," she said.

"Natasha?" Sam asked in surprise. "What the hell are you doing here? Where is Indie, and Gary?"

"They're in the bedroom," came another voice, and Sam spun in shock. There, just behind the door into the room, stood Grayson Chandler. Sam could see that his chest appeared to be heavily bandaged, but he was certainly alive. "At the moment, they're alive. Whether they stay that way or not is largely dependent on what you decide to do in the next few moments."

Kenneth Long was standing just behind Sam, his own eyes wide and unbelieving. "Natasha, Sam," he said. "She sold us out."

"I suppose you could say that," Natasha said. "I prefer to think of it as choosing the winning side. As Chandler and I were having our little talk, he told me just how complete his plans were, and that there was only one little detail he hadn't quite settled on yet."

Sam scowled at her. "Let me guess," he said. "That little detail was the final identity of the woman that he intended to put in charge, the woman who would appear to be some great Savior of the world, while he pulled the strings from behind."

"You're close," she said. "He had someone in mind, already, but it is absolutely amazing what a man will barter for his own life. No, the only little detail that wasn't settled was the matter of when all of this would be launched, and since you were already racing up here to try to stop things, I made him a simple proposition. His life in return for putting me in that top spot, and since he was ready to launch everything, anyway, we simply decided that now is the time to do it."

Sam's mind was racing, as he put together all the little details that had to fit into the scenario in front of his eyes. "Spencer," he said. "Spencer was one of yours, all along, right?"

Chandler nodded. "John has been with me for a couple of years now," he said. "Ironically, I had called him just a few hours earlier to tell him to keep his ears open for any investigators who might be snooping around the Vatican. Imagine how surprised we were when the people you called ended up calling him. He immediately figured you'd be listening in on the conversation, so he set out a bait by asking old Carlo to meet with him, knowing full well that you'd show up. Well, one of you, at least. Then he just played it by ear, telling you what you wanted to hear so that he'd be able to send you in whatever direction we wanted you sent when the time came."

"And Carlo? Is he one of yours, too?"

"No, not at all. He was just a tired old man, who didn't know who to trust."

"Was?" Sam asked. "You killed him?"

Chandler shrugged his shoulders. "Didn't have to. The thought that someone he knew might be trying to hurt the pope was more than he could take. He had a heart attack an hour after you saw him last, and I'm afraid he didn't make it."

"Okay, so let's just cut to the chase. What you want? What will it take to bargain for my wife's safety?"

Chandler smiled. "Well, I could just make you beg. Or, I could ask Natasha to give you a taste of the same treatment she gave me, that would be pretty poetic justice, wouldn't it? But don't worry, I'm not quite that vengeful. I know that all of this is nothing more than a test of my faithfulness and loyalty to Shamash, so I don't hold any grudges. No, it's a lot simpler than that, Sam. I need you on my side. I need you in particular working for me."

"And if I refuse?"

"Sam, let's not play games. If you refuse, then all four of you are going to die. That should be pretty obvious. On the other hand, if you cooperate with me, you and your wife will live and I'll even give you that computer nerd kid. I'm sure you can find a way to use his talents, so we'll put him under you. The only one who has to die is Long. And don't worry, I'm not going to make you kill him. Trust me when I say I'm going to enjoy doing that one myself."

Sam stared at Chandler for a moment, then looked at Ken. The two of them eyeballed each other for a few seconds, and then Sam turned back to Chandler. "How do I know you'll keep your word? How do I know my wife isn't dead already?"

Chandler looked at Natasha. "Would you do the honors, my dear?"

"My pleasure," Natasha said. "Just one moment." She got up from the chair she been sitting in and walked over to Sam's bedroom door. She pushed it open, and waved for someone inside to come out.

Gary and Indie came out of the room, followed by two men who were holding pistols aimed at them. Sam walked calmly over to his wife and put his arms around her, then kissed her gently. He pulled back and looked into her eyes, and then he winked.

Indie's eyes went wide, but she didn't say anything.

Sam turned away from her and looked at Chandler.

"Okay, she's alive, I see that," he said. "Since you're holding the bargaining chips, why don't we discuss this job you have for me? Mind telling me more about what it is?"

Chandler smiled, and then slowly and somewhat painfully settled himself onto a chair. "It's actually pretty simple," he said. "Basically, I need you as my personal right-hand man. Natasha will be the premier, the figurehead world ruler. I'll be sitting safely in the background, somewhere, calling the shots. When I need specific information about someone or something, you'll be the guy I turn to. With these two computer geniuses, and your own abilities as an investigator, I figure you can do just about anything I might need done along that line. In addition, the only one who will know your position will be Natasha. That way, if I need to send a message to her that can't risk going to any normal channels, I can send it to you and she'll know that it's genuine." Chandler smiled again, a shark toothed smile that made Sam nervous. "Of course, the job comes with more rewards than just your lives. You'll have wealth, power, beautiful homes in different parts of the world – you will live a life that will be the envy of millions, and all you've got to do is accept it."

Sam turned to Natasha. "Should have known I couldn't trust you," he said. "Soon as Ken said you were a former Soviet agent, I should have simply known you'd stab me in the back if you got the chance. Just out of curiosity, who else did you stab in the back? Who is supposed to get your job? Was it Sandra?"

Natasha smiled. "No, and I was surprised, myself. The woman's name was Milligan, and she was actually a pretty sharp operator. She's a British woman, a low-level staffer in the British Embassy in DC. She had been compiling information on new technologies that could solve world problems for years, and that's how Chandler stumbled across her. Don't worry about her; he's already called and let her know that she's been demoted. Like everyone else, he knows where her bodies are buried, so she's not going to raise any fuss."

"I'm sure she won't," Sam said. He turned back to Chandler. "Well, looks like you're holding all the cards. I wish I could think of a way out of this mess, but it seems you've outsmarted me."

Chandler laughed aloud. "Oh, Sam, don't feel bad," he said. "I've outsmarted more people than you can imagine. When you left me alone with Natasha down in that basement, I knew then that Shamash hadn't abandoned me or failed me. I knew that I could turn her, that I could get her to betray you. Do you know why? Do you know why I was so certain of that?"

Sam said nothing, but nodded his head. Chandler cocked his head to one side and stared at him. "Really, you think you know?" Chandler asked Sam, who nodded again. "Then, please," Chandler said with a smile, "please enlighten me. Tell me what you think the answer would be."

Sam looked at him for another moment, then said, "It's because of another prophecy. The one about Samper-shard. You figured, if that prophecy refers to me the way it seems to, then as long as I was there, I'd be winning. Once I left, though, then that prophetic influence that you felt surrounds me would be gone, and so you could use your old charm and powers of persuasion, the way you always have. Am I right?"

Chandler was still smiling, but his eyes were wide in surprise. "Actually, you're dead on the money. That was exactly it. Once you left, whatever power you had over me was removed, so she began to listen to what I had to say." He leaned forward and whispered conspiratorially. "Just between you and me, she was pretty easy to turn."

Ken was still standing just inside the doorway, and Natasha had returned to her chair. Gary and Indie had come into the room far enough to stand beside the table where their computers were set up, and their two guards were standing just a few feet away from them, with their guns still aimed loosely in their direction. Chandler had seated himself in one of the easy chairs in the sitting room, and Sam had moved to place himself directly in front of the madman.

"Natasha," Sam said, "you were easy to turn against me? Is that true?"

Natasha smiled at Sam's back. "But of course I was," she said. "After all, wasn't that our agreement, Sam?"

Chandler's smile faltered, and his eyes went wide. He moved suddenly to bring his gun to bear on Natasha, trying to lean around Sam to do so, but that's when he noticed that the two guards suddenly had their own pistols pointed directly at him. Sam leaned forward and snatched the gun from his grasp, spinning it deftly to point right back between his eyes.

"But this is impossible!" Chandler shouted. "I beat you, I had beaten you!"

Natasha stood and stepped up beside Sam, to look down at Chandler. "You know, Chandler, when Harry Winslow told me he was sending a civilian private investigator to Jerusalem to put a stop to your plans, well, I'll be honest, I thought the old man had finally lost his mind." She looked at Sam appraisingly, then turned her eyes back to Chandler. "The more I worked with him, though, the more respect I had for the natural intelligence of this man. While Kenneth and I were thinking like spies, like secret agents, like any of those other cliché words you might want to think of, Sam Prichard was thinking like an investigator. He was looking at all you have accomplished, not the way we would, thinking in terms of international incidents, or the potential for war – he looked at it as a series of crimes, and while we were trying to spot the opportunity to avoid political disaster, he was looking for any flaw in your plan, something he could exploit to turn it against you, and when we knew we had the chance to get you within our grasp, he saw one that was too good to turn down."

Chandler was staring at her, and his mouth had fallen open. "You," he said. "While I was trying to turn you against him, he was using you against me."

Natasha smiled and nodded. "Oh, indeed he did. While he and I were waiting for you to flush out of that building, he hit me with his proposition. He asked me point blank if I thought I could handle you alone, and that's when I had to tell him about my — shall we say — specialty. Then he proposed that I torture you only far enough to get you to the point of desperation, while he left me alone with you so that you would try to turn me. He suggested that I demand the number one position, that you'd be willing to trade that for your life, and it was his idea that I make you call Miss Milligan on my own phone, so that I would have not only evidence that she really was your planned puppet, but since he'd also suggested I have all of the activity on my phone traced, that call led our agents straight to her. She was in custody, with a complete news blackout on it, before you and I came up the elevator. And incidentally, she has squealed her little brains out, giving up everyone she knew that was involved in your plans." She smiled again, then stepped closer and leaned down to kiss Chandler on the cheek. "And, just so you know, it was also Sam's idea for me to demand that you give me access to your dead man's stash, so that if anything happened to you, I could keep control over the rest of your cronies. I'm delighted to be able to tell you that my phone was on full bug status as you gave me the access codes for it all, and homeland security now has complete copies of it. So, all of those high-powered politicians from around the world that you've been protecting and manipulating all this time? Well, let's just say that they're all likely to rue the day they ever even heard of you. Chandler, you bragged a few moments ago that you outsmarted so many people. Well, it just delights me to be able to tell you that Sam Prichard outsmarted you."

Chandler was staring at Sam. "You — you really are the bright one, aren't you? You really are Sam-per-shard."

Sam shrugged. "I don't know about that," he said. "When Natasha called me to tell me you had died, well, that was our signal that you had taken the bait. I knew that by the time I got to Rome, you'd already have gotten word to your people here, so when John Spencer was so anxious to be helpful, I suspected he must be one of yours. I'll grant you, I fell for the wild goose chase, I actually thought that, to keep me from suspecting, they really did have a man hunt going on for people who might have had access to the pope, so I went down to the police station expecting to really interrogate someone who may or may not have been one of yours. When I realized that it was just a decoy game to get me away from Indie and Gary, well, then I could only pray that Natasha had things under control." He looked over at his wife, smiled, and then looked back at Chandler. "I'm happy to say that, unlike yours, my God answers prayers."

Three minutes later, the room was filled with agents from the CIA and a couple of other alphabet soup groups Sam had never heard of before. Chandler was taken into custody, and Kenneth Long was delighted when he was informed that, by order of the President of the United States, he was to escort Chandler to a special holding facility that was set up specifically to house arrestees who were charged with high treason. Along with that order came a presidential pardon, one that had been hastily arranged and signed at the insistence of an extremely irate Harry Winslow, and another order reinstating Long as a special agent of the United States.

Ken came to Sam before he left with his prisoner and their escort, and shook his hand. "Sam," he said, "I gotta tell you that I thought you were nuts when we first met. And I'll even be honest enough to tell you that I still thought you were nuts as we were headed for DC together. But, buddy, if I ever have to go into another situation like this, I'm going to come drag your ass out of retirement. Just out of curiosity, though, when was it you were going to get around to telling me about this little plan you and Natasha came up with?"

Sam grinned. "When I knew whether or not it worked. You don't think I would've admitted to it if it failed, do you?"

The two men wished each other the best, and Ken told Sam not to be surprised if he showed up at the Prichard house one day soon. He was making plans to visit his daughter, and said he just didn't think he could handle coming to Denver and not seeing the best friend he'd ever known.

Sam was surprised when little Gary walked up to him, reared back and punched him right in the face. He was still staring at the kid when Gary said, "I don't know if you just thought this was funny or what, but coming face to face with that man, after you had told me he was dead, just damn near gave me a heart attack! And if you had all this all set up, why in the world did you even need me here?"

"First off, bringing you wasn't my idea, it was Harry's. And we did need you, it was your genius that managed to tap the phones that led us to John Spencer, so you did good, kid. As for you coming face-to-face with Chandler, well, let's just say I wasn't expecting that one either. When I saw him here, and you and Indie were nowhere in sight, my own heart just about failed. I'm sorry you got scared, but I think you can safely say you earned any gray hairs you got out of it."

Indie wrapped her arms around Gary in a hug, and smiled at Sam. "Just so you know, Sam, when those people came bursting in with their guns in their hands, Gary jumped in front of me. He was willing to give his life to try to save me. I think you can go a little easier on him, don't you?"

Sam looked at Gary, and smiled. "Go easier on him? I think I'm going to demand that he gets a medal!"

The debriefing lasted only a few days, and then Sam

and Indie were able to go back home. George and the limousine picked them up at the airport, and drove them to Sam's mother's house, so they could collect their daughter. Of course, that meant also collecting all of the new toys, stuffed animals, and video games her grandmothers had bought for her. George happily loaded it all into the car's huge trunk, and then he drove the family home.

It took a few days for things to settle down, and then Sam started rehearsing with the band again. Like many of the things he'd been through in his life, Sam expressed his feelings by writing them into a song. The song he wrote after this adventure got him a standing ovation when it debuted at their next concert.

Free Man

I look around my country and my tears began to fall

For the freedoms that we all once knew, Lord, we've almost lost them all

But deep within my heart I swear, I'll never be a slave,

Before this free man wears their chains, they'll put me in my grave,

Our fathers came here long ago to escape from tyranny,

And they built a mighty nation with a plan to keep it

free,

But I watch our Constitution being trampled on the ground,

Behind the noise in the voices, there's a call to make a choice, can't you hear that trumpet sound?

Chorus

So I'll stand to defend my country,

And I'll stand up for the truth,

And I'll stand as a shield to freedom,

And I'll never back down, I'll never turn and run,

I want my country back, I'm a free man!

Each night before I close my eyes, I get down on my knees,

And ask God to bless this nation and to help us keep it free,

But as long as those in power leave the law out of their plans,

And put themselves above it, they'll destroy this once great land,

For the sake of all that we hold dear, it's time to make a stand!

Chorus

So I'll stand to defend my country,

And I'll stand up for the truth,
And I'll stand as a shield to freedom,
You can't chain a free man, freedom's in his heart,
I want my country back, I'm a free man!

So I'll stand to defend your country,
And I'll stand up for the truth,
And I'll stand as a shield to freedom,
And I'll never back down, I'll never turn and run,
I want my freedoms back, I'm a free man!

BOOK 9
THE LAST SONG

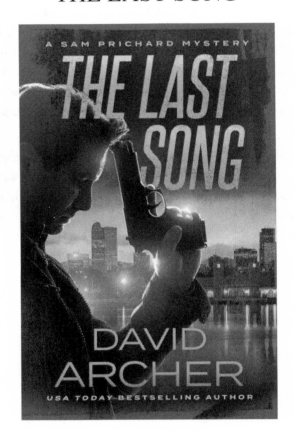

ABOUT

David Archer was born and raised in Bakersfield, California. He is a fiction author and novelist, writing in the mysteries and thrillers genre. His approach to writing is to hit deep, keep you entertained, and leave you wanting MORE with every turn of the page. He writes mysteries, thrillers, and suspense novels, all of which are primed to get your heart pumping.

The author's books are a mixture of mystery, action, suspense, and humor. If you're looking for a good place to start, take a look at his bestselling Sam Prichard Novels, available now. You can grab copies in eBook, Audio, or Paperback on all major retailers.

Made in the USA
Coppell, TX
09 May 2020